SALT OF THE NATION

Salt of the Nation

A novel
by

MATT BLOOM

Adelaide Books
New York / Lisbon
2019

SALT OF THE NATION
A novel
By Matt Bloom

Published by Adelaide Books, New York / Lisbon
adelaidebooks.org
Editor-in-Chief
Stevan V. Nikolic

For any information, please address Adelaide Books
at info@adelaidebooks.org
or write to:
Adelaide Books
244 Fifth Ave. Suite D27
New York, NY, 10001

ISBN-10: 1-950437-27-2
ISBN-13: 978-1-950437-27-6

Printed in the United States of America

To Shelley

Chapter 1

Freehold, NJ (Day 1)

Harry McBride hunched over the lunch counter and imagined he could see the ache pulsing through his right hand. He flinched when he flexed it–not from the sharp pain that caused, but from Busboy behind him shouting, *"Pow! Harry McBride!"* in a shrill, teenaged voice.

Harry swiveled his stool just enough to eye the lanky kid through his drugstore aviators. He faced forward again and pulled the bill of his Yankee cap lower, then touched his beard and regretted not having enough time to shave it off.

"Pow's right," Burger Eater said, from three stools down.

Harry returned his swollen hand to his lap and wished he could somehow trade lives with Busboy or Burger Eater, even with Waitress, who finally wandered over, boredom dulling her eyes.

"Can I getcha?" she said after maneuvering a wad of gum into her left cheek.

Harry preferred steak but chose the pulled pork sandwich to avoid gripping utensils. He inspected Waitress's ass as she plodded toward the kitchen with his order, then the skull-shaped grease spot seeping through his paper placemat–anything to keep his mind off what he'd done and his eyes off Golden Bell Diner's TV showing it once again.

Waitress returned with the sandwich, almost too quickly.

"You serve beer?" Harry mumbled to disguise his voice.

"Bud, Miller, Coors. Imported, we got Heineken." The woman seemed irritated that Harry hadn't ordered it with his food.

"Bud. Make it two…thanks."

Waitress went for the beer and Harry lifted the sandwich and bit through soft potato bun into the moist, reddish-brown pork between it. He closed his eyes and savored that first bite, the vinegary sauce tanging his nostrils, the sweet, smoky meat transporting him to a happy, care-free place far from this dreary south Jersey diner and even farther from himself.

Grover Budd's lips nearly touched the microphone as he spoke in the dulcet tone he used to at once soothe and inflame his millions of listeners.

"Question of the day, Americans: Where's Harry McBride? Where'd Harry go after punching Joe Landon off the Sargeant Gravel plant loading dock in *bea-u-ti-ful* Hackettstown, New Joisey? If anyone knows, please do your civic duty and speak up. Because Harry's out there amongst you. Maybe he *is* you. Are you listening, Harry? Good chance you are, since the Grover Budd Show happens to be the most widely syndicated radio program in the entire nation. Hey, it ain't bragging if you speak the truth."

Budd looked through the studio glass at John Willoughby in the control room, his producer's ashen complexion and blood-shot eyes symptoms of yet another beer-scotch night.

"I'm sure you've all seen it by now," Budd said, pointing a finger gun at his temple and pulling the trigger. "If for some reason you haven't, turn on your TV or your computer and watch a working stiff named Harry McBride slug Joseph P. Landon, US senator from Idaho, presidential candidate, and true blue Republican. Case in point: Senator Landon's voted to repeal universal healthcare *sixty-two times*. Sixty-two courageous stands against Big Government trampling our right to live in a free country built by free enterprise."

Budd crossed his eyes at Willoughby. Willoughby crossed his back.

"This Harry McBride character disturbs me," Budd continued. "I mean, is it possible Socialist Barry Schwartz or some revamped version of Occupy Wall Street is what inspired him? Sure. Could he be part of a radical Islamic terrorist cell? Perhaps. But the most likely and frightening scenario, as far as I'm concerned, is the wine-sipping scoundrels commonly known as the Democrat Party offered McBride a fair amount of dough to punch the good senator right in the old schnozola. I just know deep in my ample gut that's what happened." Budd winked at Willoughby. "And guess what, Americans? You know it, too."

Calvin Evans remained seated in the front pew even though the morning service in Grace Baptist Church of Alexandria had ended and all the "Brunch-Eaters" had left. Let them go stuff their pie holes with bacon and eggs and pancakes, Evans thought of his fellow worshippers. I'll stay right here and keep feeding on what won't end up in the toilet.

"Taking Off The Gloves," Pastor Johnson's sermon encouraging beleaguered Christian Americans to resist their persecutors by embracing the Scriptures, had brought un-abashed tears to Evans's eyes. When not quietly weeping, he'd scrutinized the congregation through misty eyes, contemptuous of those who'd appeared less moved by the pastor's words. He suspected this dangerous faithlessness had been spawned and spread by the seemingly harmless technology and social media now saturating the country–smartphones and internet, Facebook and Twitter–these just some of Satan's soul-suckers. Evans had always believed Rock and Roll to be the most potent and insidious satanic weapon of all, the one that had created the chink in America's armor through which the Korean War, Vietnam, 9-11, Iraq, Afghanistan, all those hurricanes, even ISIS, had invaded. One after another after another. Oh, the demise of a once promising nation. The promised land, Evans thought. *If only.*

He meshed his fingers, closed his eyes, and resumed praying.

The overweight youth sucked down a milkshake in one of Golden Bell's side booths, his close-set, bespectacled eyes glued to an iPhone streaming a YouTube video of Harry McBride belting Senator Landon.

"Guy musta been a boxa or somethin'," the kid said to no one in particular.

Busboy snapped a damp rag at the back of Burger Eater's neck on his way to wipe a table.

"Pow! Harry McBride!"

Burger Eater seemed too absorbed by the TV news to notice the rag attack.

"That McBride guy sure can punch."

Harry ducked slightly when Youth in The Booth looked up from his phone and squinted in his direction. He nearly plugged his ears when Waitress aimed the clicker at the TV and raised the volume.

"*...who earlier today assaulted Senator Joe Landon while Landon was campaigning...*" the Fox News anchorman was saying. "*Mr. Landon is currently in St. Barnabas hospital undergoing tests for a possible concussion, having reportedly sustained a broken nose and tailbone. Mr. McBride is still at large...*"

Harry scanned the diner for threats he might have missed, then examined his placemat again. He noticed the skull-shaped grease spot had spread and appeared to be smiling at him now; a mirthless, knowing smile.

Grover Budd cleared his throat as an ad for gold coins ended. He switched on his microphone.

"Welcome back to the Grover Budd Show, Americans. As I tweeted during the break, my trusted sources have provided me with strong evidence confirming the Democrats did actually hire Harry McBride to attack Landon, either to remove him from the race or to at least make him appear weak. Whatever their specific intent, a socialist named Barry Schwartz occupies the White House for the next four years if their scheme works. *God help us!*"

Budd made a faux-horrified face at Willoughby, who held up two fingers while tilting the last of a Red Bull into his mouth.

"Speak, loyal American listener," Budd said, pushing phone line #2. "Tell Grover what's pissing you off. Tell Grover what's scaring the bejeezus out of you."

"Hi, Grover, this is Gail Cressey from Tulsa, Oklahoma, proud grandma of two wonderful young ladies."

"Congratulations, Granny Gail. What's bothering you?"

"This whole healthcare thing Landon's been fighting against is what. I'm just worried if the federal government can take over our healthcare and give it to people who aren't even real Americans, what in God's name will they take over next?"

"You hit the proverbial nail on the head, Granny G," Budd said. "What *will* the federal government confiscate next? More importantly, as you so pointedly pointed out, who the heck will they let into our country to take advantage of it? Let's talk about that…"

Calvin Evans considered his recent lack of work to be part of God's plan, His test, His way of strengthening and improving him through hardship and trial, the same way He created the finest wines from the most stringent soils. The wine analogy resonated with Evans despite having swapped alcohol for religion ten years ago. He still considered that exchange to have been a major watershed in his life. Because, as if by magic, his middling career in the FBI began to flourish soon afterward, mainly free of the close encounters with department regulations resulting from his often off-the-book methods. And his subsequent involvement in several high-profile cases—most notably saving Senator Landon's then college-aged daughter from the People's Power cult—earned him acclaim and a promotion.

Though try as he might, Evans could never escape the fact that rescuing one young woman had boosted his professional life just as swiftly as his encounter with another had destroyed it. The girl central to his downfall had been alive for exactly sixteen years and three days when Evans had approached her at the Landmark Mall, in Alexandria, Virginia. This had made the sex he'd had with her while on duty fully legal, according to Virginia state law. FBI rules, on the other hand, proved more puritanical. So, when the girl broke her agreed-to silence about Evans luring her to the nearby Motel 6 on Springfield Boulevard, Evans's boss demanded his badge and sent him packing.

"I know I'm weak, Lord," Evans whispered, his eyes aimed at the floor. "All I'm asking for is a little strength."

He pushed himself to his feet, adjusted the shoulder holster strapped beneath his blazer, and walked purposely up the aisle. Aware that receiving favor from God required advance payment, he left the empty church and circled around back, where he found Will Dunning smoking a cigarette.

The porter pulled a final drag and flicked the butt.

"You don't have to do this again, Mr. Evans."

"Oh, I most certainly do, Will."

Dunning rolled his eyes, the whites contrasting sharply with dark brown lids.

"If you insist."

"You people have been doing this type of work for years," Evans said. "Who am I not to?"

"All I'm sayin' is I wouldn't if I didn't have to, Mr. Evans."

"Call me Calvin, Will. Calvin…please."

The ex-FBI agent grasped the mop protruding from the yellow wheeled bucket Dunning had already filled with warm water and pine solution. He gave Dunning a solemn look of solidarity before pushing on the handle and guiding the bucket into the church.

Burger Eater dabbed a fry into a puddle of ketchup.

"McBride's gotta set of balls. I'll give him that."

"Harry's gonna break the internet." Youth in the Booth had become one with his iPhone again. "Awesome!"

"Pow! Harry McBride!"

Burger Eater rotated his stool and pointed his ketchup-ed fry at Busboy.

"Stop fuckin' sayin' that."

"Watch your mouth!" Waitress barked.

Burger Eater faced forward again and ate the fry.

"This'll be the best job you ever have if you keep acting like a jerkoff," he told Busboy once Waitress had moved beyond earshot. "Clearin' dishes like an illegal Mexican."

"At least I *got* a job." Busboy laughed and smacked his palm again. *"Pow!"*

"Two million six hundred and twenty-seven YouTube views so far," Youth in The Booth said, a grin now bunching his pudgy cheeks. "Cray-zee."

Waitress returned and jerked her chin at the TV.

"He's sexy…in an ugly kinda way."

"You *would* think that," Burger Eater said.

"Don't get me wrong, I hope they catch the bastard," Waitress said.

Burger Eater excavated a hunk of burger and spoke while chewing it.

"Can't really blame him for what he did."

Busboy put down his tray and started dancing right behind Harry.

"Go, Harry, go! Go, Harry, go!"

Harry hoped Busboy's tuneless chanting and rhythm-less dancing is what had inspired Waitress to direct a frown across the diner toward him. The frown made him uneasy regardless of its target, and he would have left if not for the remainder of his second Budwieser. The beer tasted especially good, and its gentle buzz had eased some of his anxiety. The buzz vanished and his anxiety returned full-force when a car commercial segued back to Fox News, now featuring the anchorman and a sandy-haired man in a lab coat occupying opposite sides of a split-screen.

"I'm joined by Dr. Richard Smith, chief neurologist at St. Barnabas Medical Center, in Livingston, New Jersey, where Senator Landon was taken after the assault. Welcome, Dr. Smith. I know you're a busy man right now, but if you wouldn't mind taking a look at the crime and discussing the head injury Landon suffered today as a result of it."

Fox replayed the punch, pausing footage just as Harry's fist greeted Senator Landon's nose. Harry couldn't resist peeking. *Not a bad punch,* he thought. He nearly laughed at his co-workers' astonished expressions and at Landon's Secret Service detail, stiff as mannequins in the moment before their failed attempt to tackle him.

Perched on that shaky diner stool, Harry's back felt as stiff as the Secret Service looked. Shoveling gravel five days a week for twenty-one years will do that, same as it did to his father. Harry had joined his old man at Sargeant soon after being expelled from high school for fighting one too many times. Defending himself and others is how Harry saw it.

The gravel he trailed his father into eventually became quicksand, trapping him in the job and in the town, his prospects of escape diminishing with each year spent swinging that big scoop shovel, with each year keeping the endless stream of pulverized stone flowing into the chute. Harry had tried to work up to more cushy positions at the plant: crusher operator, truck driver. He'd even tried to find a job at Mars Chocolate, headquartered right there in Hackettstown. But no one at Mars showed any interest in Harry's skill-set, and no one at Sargeant could imagine him handling anything other than a shovel.

Working all day with earplugs blocking any chance to converse did allow Harry time to think, even to dream. Of being a poet, of all things. The ambition had always struck him as odd, the same way a dog that yearns to fly might. He'd heard of working-class bards such as Charles Bukowski, but had never actually read any of them. Still, he felt things that seemed worth saying, and poems giving voice to those things would emerge from time to time. He wrote down as many as possible, whenever he could, making sure to never show them to his co-workers. Life at the plant was tough enough.

And his back steadily worsened as the years progressed, eventually defying the Percocet that had once transported him to a fuzzy, pain-free float. Increasing doses of alcohol had filled the gap left by the drug's waning powers, but only until it too failed to do the trick. By the time New Jersey's governor had cut aid to those fighting addictions, Harry had found himself trapped by and eventually alone with his, the pain haunting him like an evil spirit.

To avoid dwelling on his back, Harry tried to summon remorse for what he'd done earlier that day, even sympathy for the man he'd done it to. He rubbed his own once-broken jaw, but the trace of remorse and compassion that conjured proved no match for his memory of Landon on the loading dock, spouting something about hard work and self-reliance paving the road to the American Dream.

Landon's speech had tripped an alert in Harry's highly-calibrated bullshit detector, specifically the part about hard work. *The fuck you think I do here all day long?* The irritation that particular statement had sparked had built into anger that had caused sweat rivulets to form on Harry's temples and trickle into his beard. The portion of the speech decrying government assistance as the first step toward dependency had revved Harry's internal engine even higher, eventually folding his fingers into fists. *What the hell's wrong with helping people?* Then the obligatory hand-shaking as Landon had made his way down the line of gravel workers, fake smile plastered on his face. Harry knew the smile is what had done it, what had pushed him over the edge. Nothing worse than a smile from the guy trying to stick it to you.

"…It wasn't just a punch, it was a declaration of war," Grover Budd told a new caller. "Not a war against terror in the Middle East, but one right here against America, waged by the freedom-quashing Democrat Party, a far more dangerous foe, in my humble opinion."

John Willoughby finished rubbing his eyes and held up three fingers. Budd thanked Mike from Phoenix and pushed line #3.

"Speak, loyal listener. Tell Grover what's got your knickers in a twist today."

"Thanks for taking my call, Grover. This is Thierry, from To-peka, Kansas, and my knickers are just fine. In fact, they're in better shape than they've been in a long time."

"Are you calling from a psychiatric ward, Thierry? Because it seems the only ones who feel good these days are clinically insane."

"I'm perfectly sane, Grover. And I'm sure I speak for millions of other perfectly sane Americans who are elated for precisely the reason you're so up in arms."

"Wow, you're quite a fancy talker, Thierry. I thought all elitists lived on the coasts. "

"Well, to us so-called Midwest elitists, Harry McBride's a hero who I suspect is equally fed up with Republicans like Landon

working for the rich and powerful while selling the rest of the country down the river."

"Kansas," Budd said. "The great state that's given us amber waves of grain, Dorothy, and the Wicked Witch of the West. Seems it's also given us Thierry, a man whose head is so far up his own kiester he can actually see his tonsils." Budd closed line #3. "Sorry, Americans. Don't know how that one slipped past Willoughby into our world. Too much boozin' last night, John? Back after these."

Budd cut the mike and grinned while thinking of his Wizard of Oz reference and his dig at Willoughby's drinking. His grin proved fleeting, though, chased by the daily migraine sprouting between his eyes, poised to spread across his forehead and squeeze his temples in its ever-tightening vice.

Calvin Evans wheeled the bucket back behind the church after he'd finished mopping its floor.

"Clean as a whistle," he told Will Dunning, who leaned against a dented green dumpster, smoking another cigarette.

Dunning laughed, exposing tobacco-stained teeth.

"If you think moppin' a church gonna give you a speed pass through the Pearly Gates, then that's your right."

Evans forced a smile.

"Hopefully I don't get to those gates too soon. As always, thanks for the opportunity. See you next week?"

"I wouldn't bet on anything different."

"Just keep your betting rhetorical, Will. Most gambling's illegal for a reason, ya know."

Evans made sure to look the African-American in the eye while shaking his hand; acknowledge his humanity the way he would any white person's. He left Dunning and headed to his Dodge Caravan in the front lot, tired and mellowed from all the listening and praying and mopping he'd done that morning. But his hard-earned serenity shattered as soon as he got in the minivan and looked at the Barely Legal magazine in the passenger seat, a beautiful teenaged girl wearing only a pout gracing its cover. *Oh, sweet, wicked girl.* Evans gaped at her until he summoned enough will to fling the dog-eared periodical into the back seat, revealing the King James Bible beneath it. He grabbed the Book, frantically flipped to James 1:12, and read it aloud:

"Blessed is the man who endures temptation; for when he has been approved, he will receive the crown of life..."

Evans closed the Bible, somewhat calmed and fortified by the passage. He wiped the sweat from his brow and started the Caravan with no particular destination in mind. His phone rang before he could drive off, the caller ID indicating "Joseph Landon."

Harry McBride made sure no one had tailed him from Golden Bell Diner before wending through its parking lot and stopping at the edge of NJ Route 9. The cars on the highway blurred before his tired eyes, their perpetual motion and rhythmic whooshing almost hypnotic. His cell phone vibrated as he waited for traffic to break.

"Grace."

"Oh, Harry."

Harry pictured the disapproving expression that always made his ex-wife's face even prettier.

"Yeah, I know."

"I'm afraid to ask."

"He made us miss our game."

"He probably did you a favor."

"I was on a winning streak."

"Let me get this straight. You punched a senator because he made you miss your lunchtime poker."

Harry smiled thinking of how he'd won big the day before Landon's visit, how he'd laid a royal flush on the table just as the break whistle had blown.

"I was getting hungry, too," he said. "They put us through all kinds of security, then forced us to wait hours for that prick to finally show."

"Jesus, Harry, you never change."

Harry flexed his right hand as far as the pain allowed.

"I been more depressed than usual, tell ya the truth. Layoffs at Sargeant making me nervous, and their insurance don't cover my meds no more, thanks to douchebags like Landon."

"I'm sure that's not his fault."

"I don't care if it is or not. It's what he stands for."

Grace sighed.

"You have to stop being so angry."

Harry checked behind him, half expecting to find a police officer or even Busboy there. He felt badly for the dopy kid, having to work such a crappy job with such crappy people. He felt even worse for the one in the booth and almost wished he could go back inside and tell him to stop drinking milkshakes and staring at his goddamn phone all the time. *Get some exercise, for crissakes!*

"Lemme ask ya, Grace, what have people like Landon ever done for people like us except use us in photo-ops every four years?"

"What do you want them to do?"

"To stop taking things away."

"Things. What things?"

"Our jobs, our healthcare, our…they'll steal whatever they can get their hands on is what I'm saying."

"And this was your revenge."

"Why should I always be the one taking shit?"

"We all take shit. Come back and turn yourself in."

"I don't know."

Grace sighed again.

"The cops and the FBI, even some weird-sounding PI named Calvin or Calvert, been calling me."

"Don't tell 'em nothing."

"I'm not stupid, Harry." Grace went silent, then said, *"Christ, why'd you have to go and do this?"*

Harry searched for an answer while marveling at a seagull floating effortlessly above him, invisible currents keeping it aloft.

"Hey, can you say that word I like?"

"Which word?"

"The one you made up the time we were really drunk at McNally's."

"Schportles?"

"*Schportles.* I love that."

"It's not even a word."

"That's why it cracks me up."

Grace chuckled.

"Listen, you better hang up before they track your phone or something."

"All right. I'll try to call later."

Harry ended the call and his spirits sank again without Grace's voice buoying them. He scurried through a gap in traffic to the giant mall parking lot on the other side of Route

9. There he found the Ford Taurus he'd hotwired after escaping Sargeant, got in, and sat behind the wheel trying to review his still-vague plan to somehow reach and cross the Mexican border. Then what? he wondered as a wave of sadness for what he'd lost and what he'd never have washed over him. He started the car once the wave passed, then switched on the radio. It happened to be tuned to the Grover Budd Show.

"...You can run, McBride, but you can't hide," Budd was saying. *"Give me a call, Harry. 1-800-575-2900. We'll chat and figure this out..."*

Harry killed the radio and eased out of the spot. He drove slowly through the parking lot, past Best Buy and Appleby's and Home Depot, their familiarity stark reminders of the unfamiliar turn his life had taken. He braked at the mall exit, and while waiting for the light, he considered heeding Grace's advice; heading north to Hackettstown and surrendering to the authorities. He instead turned south when red went green, determined to drive all night without stopping, fast beyond reach of the nation and the long, grasping fingers of his own sorrow and fear.

Chapter 2

Senator Joe Landon couldn't decide if his face or his ass felt worse, only that both hurt like hell. And while he imagined the plastic mask protecting his fractured nose made him look somewhat tough, he feared walking all stiff and tentative as a result of his busted tailbone might create the opposite impression. If fifteen years of public service had taught him anything, it's the American voter has little mercy for the weak and wounded.

Although no fan of FDR and his New Deal, Landon did grudgingly admire the former president's grit and ability to conceal his polio. Easier to do back then, of course. Franky D didn't exactly have a 24-hour cable news cycle or the internet or smart phone cameras to contend with. Nor did he have the phony Liberal Media proclaiming all his deeds and intentions to be Satan's work, even concocting things out of thin air. *Well, none of that's going to beat Joe Landon.*

Pain shot through the nerves connecting his butt to his hips when he shifted in his hospital bed. He looked at his wife, perched on the sill, gazing out the window as if considering a jump. Landon knew Ellen hated the campaign; the countless stops, the talking to reporters and voters, the having to smile all the time. He often reminded her that this journey he'd embarked on was bigger and more important than the both of them. He sometimes wondered if she bought it.

While admiring Ellen's silvering but still lustrous hair, the shallow crow's feet giving her character and gravitas, he couldn't help recalling their first date senior year in high school. *To Kill a Mockingbird* had just ended, leaving Gregory Peck's Atticus Finch entrenched in young Landon's heart and mind, inspiring him to do great things for the rest of his life. He felt an overwhelming need to tell Ellen about it right there in the front seat of his dad's Buick.

So he did!

Ellen had laughed when Landon proclaimed he'd be president of the United States one day. Landon had recoiled at his future wife's reaction, but her laughter also became a prime motivator driving his long political career; one created by his desire to help the country the way Attitus Finch had helped the poor negro, yet sustained by his need to prove Ellen wrong, to turn her long-ago laughter back on itself.

He glanced at Chris Watkins and thought he detected an undercurrent of mirth on his campaign manager's boyish face. *Think getting walloped on national TV and looking like a bedridden hockey goalie is funny, Chris?* He focused on his sore nose to avoid dwelling on his damaged pride.

"What's the plan, Chris?"

The hint of amusement fled Watkins's face. He flicked lint off the sleeve of his navy Calvin Klein suit.

"We obviously can't undo what's already happened," he said. "So, we'll have to work with it."

"Work with what?"

"I think we create a new narrative for you. Get this: Joe Landon: Victim."

Landon shifted again and gritted his teeth against a fresh wave of discomfort.

"Joe Landon: Victim?"

"Not just at the Sargent Gravel plant, but for your entire life."

"Wait a minute, did you just say '*victim*?'"

"Americans love them," Watkins said. "Look how popular Reagan became after he was shot. No one says a bad word about Lincoln or Kennedy or the other one who got killed. How about Joe Landon: Perpetual Victim?"

"I don't know."

Watkins crossed his legs knee over knee.

"Here's the twist. Joe Landon, perpetual victim who's not only overcome all his hardships and enemies, but who's forgiven each and every one of them, including Harry McBride. Joe Landon: Magnanimous Perpetual Victim."

"Don't people like winners, not victims?"

"We have to work with what we have, Joe. It's called spin."

Landon hated when Watkins spoke down to him like that. *Just remember who's boss, Mr. Ivy League Nancy Boy.*

"I suppose you could say Dick Nixon always portrayed himself as a victim."

"Good example."

Landon glanced at Ellen and wondered if she preferred looking out the window to looking at him.

"What do you think, Ellen?"

Ellen turned and gave Landon a brittle smile.

"What do I think about what?"

"Joe Landon, perpetual magnanimous victim?"

"*Magnanimous* perpetual victim," Watkins corrected. "Maybe we cut perpetual."

Ellen seemed to give it some thought, although lately Landon couldn't tell when Zoloft had merely floated her to a placid, thought-free cloud.

"Sounds fine," she said. "But do you really consider yourself a victim? And how about Tibbens, your faithful running mate?"

Landon ignored Ellen's sarcasm.

"We'll make Earl a victim, too." He smiled painfully. "We're *all* victims, Ellen. You, me, Earl, Chris…every single American's a victim one way or another."

"I feel your pain," Watkins said, mimicking Bill Clinton's lazy Ozark accent.

Landon snapped his fingers.

"That smarmy sonofabitch had the right idea, though. Turn on the news, Mr. and Mrs. American, and watch Joe Landon literally feeling your pain on that Sargent Gravel plant loading dock."

"Fucking genius," Watkins said.

"Language, Chris."

"Sorry, Joe. Sorry, Ellen."

But Ellen had already faced the window again, seemingly oblivious to Watkins' curse.

"Then, when they see me back on the campaign trail looking a little worse for wear, they'll say, 'Sure, Joe Landon got knocked down. But he got right back on his feet. One tough sonofagun.'"

Watkins clapped his hands.

"What I particularly like is it's layered. You're not only a victim, which every American can relate to, but you persevere, which every American admires. *And* you forgive your assailant, demonstrating what a truly spiritual and kind-hearted man you are."

Landon angled his body toward Watkins, sending more hurt into his hip.

"Kind-hearted, sure. The problem with spiritual is I haven't been going to church that much."

"Go more often. And talk about it."

"Let me play devil's advocate here. This Harry McBride guy went postal on me for no apparent reason. Truth be told, I hope they catch the asshole and he rots in jail. Wouldn't forgiving him be telling voters I'm not concerned with law and order?"

"I didn't say pardon him or drop charges," Watkins said. "I said *forgive* him. Demonstrate that you feel sorry for the sick bastard. Joe Landon, tough on crime, a man who fights back, but also a compassionate forgiver."

"Compassionate forgiver. What do you think, Ellen?"

"Sounds good to me," Ellen said, before whispering something unintelligible to the window pane.

Watkins pinched his chin between his thumb and index finger.

"We'll have to work Harry McBride into the story just the right way. The first question is why did he slug you?"

"How the hell should I know?"

"Nothing you might have done to aggravate him?"

Landon shrugged.

"Maybe he's mentally ill."

"No, he's not mentally ill," Watkins said, a gleam coming into his eyes. "He slugged you because he's an average American who's sick and tired."

"Sick and tired of what?"

"Of politicians and lobbyists, of backroom deals and huge corporations getting all the breaks while they cheat and exploit people like him. He's sick and tired of all that and he's sick and tired of being sick and tired."

"So, he saw *me* as everything he's sick and tired of."

Watkins stood, as if to make a speech.

"Harry McBride's a simple, working-class man who mistakenly conflated you with all that's bad and corrupt in this country. And he expressed that the only way he knew how. I mean, he doesn't seem the type to submit an op-ed to the New York Times."

"Certainly not."

Watkins sat again and meshed his fingers around his knee.

"Don't take this the wrong way, Joe, but getting punched by McBride might have been the best thing could have happened to you."

"Let's switch places and see if you say that."

"What I mean is it's given us the opportunity to change your image and convince voters you're no run-of-the-mill Beltway insider. We play it right and Harry McBride can take us all the way to the White House."

The White House. Old 1600 Pennsylvania Avenue. Landon had been there several times since becoming Idaho's junior senator, in 1994. Bill Clinton had been the most fun to visit. Hard not to like the guy or laugh at his stories and jokes despite his willingness to rip any Republican to shreds if given half a chance. Meeting with George W. Bush was like hanging with a brother in the world's premier frat house. "Mo Joe," is the nickname W had given Landon, one Ellen had started using until Joe told her to knock it off. Landon still didn't know what to make of or feel about Obama; he still couldn't quite get his mind around a black man with a Muslim name in the Oval Office, for two terms no less. Granted, this particular black man acted fairly American and Christian and white, except when he played basketball and gave speeches in that Martin Luther King Jr. cadence of his. Not that acting traditionally black is necessarily a bad thing, Landon reminded himself.

Regardless, he felt sure a black man in the White House had been a mere historical anomaly, a footnote that would inevitably be followed by a return to normalcy represented by none other than Joe Landon. He had little doubt his well-earned turn was at hand, and being punched off the loading dock by a deranged gravel worker may have been his final dues payment. He decided he'd let Ellen make all the redecorating decisions once they occupied the big house; his gift to her for enduring the long ride there. He imagined her waking each morning with rekindled light in her eyes. *I told you I'd get here, Ellen. You laughed at me all those years ago, but I told you.*

Landon checked the wall clock.

"What do I tell them, Chris?"

"Short, sweet, and to the point. You might try a little humor, too."

"Humor's not my strong suit."

"That's why it'd have even more impact. Mention God, too, at least once. It also couldn't hurt to hint that Barry Schwartz might be behind this."

"Think he is?"

"Of course, not. That said, you really don't have to do this right now."

Landon smiled wearily.

"They're gonna get to me eventually. May as well turn the boat into enemy fire."

"You'll do fine, senator."

Watkins went to the door and exchanged a few words with the Secret Service agents stationed outside it. Landon motioned Ellen to the bedside seat and took her hand in his just as a throng of reporters and cameramen pushed past Watkins.

"Hi everyone," Landon said once they'd jostled into a scrum around his bed. "Never thought I'd be talking to you guys in a hospital wearing a Hannibal Lechter mask."

Polite chuckles.

"I'll tell you this: the other guy looks even worse."

More half-hearted laughs.

"First of all, except for a broken nose and tailbone, I'm perfectly fine. The excellent doctors here at St. Barnabas say I'll make a full recovery and the campaign will continue until I'm either defeated or I reach the White House."

Landon pretended to collect himself.

"I'm also so grateful to have my wife, Ellen, by my side. And Joe Jr. and Denise, my two wonderful children, are en route. As you may have guessed, I won't have the energy to answer all your questions individually, but I think I know what you want, so here goes: My injuries did and do hurt. I don't know who Harry McBride is except that he worked at the Sargent Gravel plant, in Hackettstown, NJ, and he's not connected to my opponent, Barry Schwartz…as far as I know."

Landon paused to review what he and Watkins had discussed.

"Make no mistake, this was a crime perpetrated by an obviously disturbed individual who *will* be brought to justice. I don't hate Harry McBride, nor do I bear him ill will. *He's* the wounded one, not me, and I hope he gets whatever help he needs once he's caught."

Landon paused again for effect.

"You know the old cliché: it's not the falling down; it's the getting back up. Well, Harry McBride and many others have knocked me down my whole life. I've gotten up each and every time and I'll continue to as leader of this great nation."

He remembered God.

"What I'm saying is God helps those who help themselves. I believe that's what the Lord wants me to do in order to help this country. Now I have a bit more recuperating to do, as you can see, so I'd appreciate if you'd all show yourselves to the door and I'll see you real soon."

Landon's attempt to avoid questions worked for about three seconds. Then…

"Have you been given any idea where Harry McBride is now, senator?"

"No idea."

"Are you on pain medication, sir?"

"Nope," Landon lied. "A life lived without some pain is a life not properly lived." He made a mental note to remember that one.

"Did Mr. McBride say anything before he punched you?"

"Not a word."

"Will there be any repercussions for Secret Service's failure to apprehend McBride at the scene?"

"We'll have to review everything before we make any decisions."

"Do you think this will help or hurt your campaign?"

Watkins pushed through the reporters before Landon could answer that one.

"All right, enough for today."

"You mentioned Barry Schwartz before," a reporter for the local NBC affiliate said, ignoring Watkins. "You indicated he wasn't involved, *as far as you knew*. Does that mean you think Schwartz *might* be involved?"

"I'm not ruling anything out," Landon said, glad the question had kept the Schwartz factor in play.

"Okay, we're finished here," Watkins said, shooing the reporters. "We'll be happy to give you more once the senator has recovered some."

Landon released Ellen's hand as soon as the room had cleared. Ellen returned to the windowsill.

"Not bad," Watkin said. "I worried you'd forgotten about God, but you pivoted nicely at the end."

"I could have gone longer."

"More important for you to rest. I'll see you tomorrow."

Watkins left and the ensuing silence between Landon and Ellen would have been uncomfortable if they weren't used to it.

"What the hell you looking out the window at, Ellen?"

The senator's wife kept her eyes on the non-descript, soot-covered building across the street.

"Nothing, honey."

"Nothing sure seems interesting."

Ellen turned to her husband.

"How you feeling, Joe?"

"Like crap."

"I'm sorry you feel like crap. I think I'll go back to the hotel and get some rest."

Ellen came over to the bed and gave her husband a quick, dry kiss atop his head.

"We're *going* to get to the White House," Landon said.

"I know you will."

Ellen left the room and Landon heard her speaking with a Secret Service agent through the closed door. He then heard Ellen's high heels and those of the agent clicking in tandem toward the elevators.

Chapter 3

Route 17 emerged from murky pre-dawn into Warrenton, Virginia's neon alley, its dual-sided row of fast food and motels and car dealerships glaring through the windshield. The town seemed like one endless strip to Harry, though no different from the others he'd already driven through that night. He felt bone tired and would have fallen asleep behind the wheel if not for the multi-colored lights assaulting his eyes and the pain dogging his hand and back.

A red and white Arbys reminded him of the hero sandwich he'd made that morning, so long ago it seemed; an inch of roast beef topped with iceberg lettuce, ripe Jersey tomato, red onion, and homemade Russian dressing. Yet instead of eating it, he'd spent his lunch break waiting to shake Senator Landon's hand for the cameras after listening to him spout phony populism for what seemed like hours. He monitored an oncoming state trooper until the cruiser passed and disappeared from the rearview. He tapped the brakes as he approached a Burger King, but defied his sharpening hunger and kept going, intent on adding miles while minimizing human contact.

Which is exactly what he'd done after slugging Senator Landon, instinctively ducking beneath the closest Secret Service agent's tackle, causing the agent to collide with the one who'd lunged at him from the other side. Both agents had fallen and three more had tripped over them in a futile effort to grab Harry.

Heavy, steel-toed boots had slowed Harry's flight, but not enough to prevent him from escaping into the maze of crushers and storage bins and gravel chutes beyond the loading dock's metal doors. The massive equipment had provided the cover he'd needed to slip unseen out the side exit few knew about, then slink across the narrow parking lot into the swamp only mosquitos and frogs and a family of muskrats called home.

The fuel gauge of the Taurus he'd stolen from a back street several blocks from Sargeant hovered near empty, forcing him to stop at an Exxon on the far side of Warrenton. He pumped gas with his Yankee cap pulled low and paid for it with some of the $400 he'd managed to withdraw from an ATM on his way out of Hackettstown. He continued south after filling up, the tuner scanning songs he'd never heard and some he'd heard thousands of times. It paused on mattress and insurance and beer commercials, and on DJs who all sounded the same. It soon landed on one who didn't.

"*…Thanks for your call, Kevin from Kentucky. KK, for short. If Kevin here happens to hail from Keaton, Kentucky, Grover Budd just might have another run-in with the almighty PC Police. But seriously, KK, you and everyone else have so far failed to address and answer the burning question of the day, which is where the hell is Harry McBride?*"

Harry froze the tuner on the Grover Budd Show rerun.

"*…Where exactly is that bearded bastard who slugged Senator Landon? Hey, Harry, where are you? Better yet, WHO are you and*

WHAT are you, and how much is Barry Schwartz, or maybe it's the Democrat Party, paying you?…"

Harry cleared Warrenton and turned onto an unlit, unmarked road three miles beyond the town line. He pulled over after rounding a bend and got out with the scissors and electric razor he'd bought at a Walgreens in Chester, Pennsylvania. He'd also purchased a map, two long-sleeved shirts, water, bread, and peanut butter. He would have bought more but feared the night clerk might remember a man stocking fugitive supplies.

Thorns and prickers grabbed at his green Dickey's as he bush-wacked through a tangle of shrubs and a stand of weed trees. He began to scissor his hair and beard in a clearing beyond them; clumps fell to the ground and scattered like pine needles around his boots still dusted with pulverized New Jersey blue stone. He ran the electric razor over his scalp and cheeks next, and returned to the car as smooth-faced and bald as an infant. He looked in the rearview and his newly-exposed lips made him feel somewhat vulnerable, although he felt pleased the jaw he hadn't seen in years still appeared chiseled.

He started the engine and Grover Budd flowed back into the car.

"…that a nobody like Harry McBride can just punch a U.S. senator is a sure sign this country's going to hell in a handbasket…"

Harry pushed "Scan" once he got back onto Route 17. The tuner abandoned Budd in favor of *Rainy Days and Mondays,* by the Carpenters, the glum melody and depressing lyrics compelling Harry to push "Scan" again. The tuner ran right back to Budd.

"…I'm talking to you, McBride. Turn yourself in and face the music…"

Harry hesitated before pulling his phone from his pocket and dialing with his thumb.

"*Harry?*"

"It's me."

"*You're not supposed to be callin'.*"

"You gotta listen to this crap, Grace."

Harry held the phone to the dashboard speaker so his ex-wife could hear Budd.

"*...Barry Schwartz and his socialist Democrat Party are using Harry McBride—and I'm sure they'll use others just like him—to start a class war for the purpose of taking wealth from those who create it and redistributing it to those who don't create a damned thing...*"

Harry brought the phone to his mouth.

"Hear what this prick's saying about me?"

"*Don't listen to him.*"

"There's nothing else on."

"*Then turn off the radio!*"

"It helps me stay awake."

"*You shouldn't be driving tired. How's your back?*"

"Barking like a dog."

"*You got your Percocet?*"

"Percocet don't work no more."

"*Well, don't drink.*"

"I only had two beers."

A pause on the other end.

"*I know I shouldn't ask, but where the hell you goin'?*"

"Mexico."

"*That's ridiculous.*"

"They said the same thing about putting a man on the moon."

"*The rocket scientists didn't go punch a senator in the face.*"

"He deserved it."

Grace yawned into the phone.

"Whatever you say. I gotta go back to sleep. One of the other nurses is sick, so I got early shift tomorrow."

"How your patients doing?"

"Most cancer patients die."

"Don't know how you do it."

"You better turn yourself in, Harry. You're already in a shit-load of–"

"I know, I know."

"Do it. And don't do nothin' stupid in the meantime."

"Stupid? *Me?*"

"Just be careful."

Grace hung up and Harry shut off the phone to save battery.

"…This is interesting," Budd said. *"The footage of McBride reveals a Pegasus tattoo on his right forearm. One of those flying horses. But get this: Harry's Pegasus not only has wings, it also a horn protruding from its forehead. Seems the man's gotten his Greek mythological creatures mixed up, which suggests he's not the sharpest tool in the shed…"*

Harry turned off the radio and took the next exit off Route 17. He followed smaller state and county roads from there, fewer lights and cars the further south and west he went. A billboard advertising a gift shop in Johnsonboro, Virginia inspired him to pull over and retrieve a pen from the glove compartment. He used it to write on the napkin he'd taken from the Golden Bell Diner, pressing gently to keep from poking through:

You gave me everything, Grace, but I was blind to your gift. Now I'm on the road with nothing, only your sweet voice giving me wisdom before your early morning shift.

He folded the napkin, closed his eyes, and imagined writing more poetry in Mexico, maybe even short stories. He pictured the sun-drenched seaside village he'd live in and the baby he and Grace might have if he could convince her to join him and that things would be different. No miscarriages down there. None of the other problems, either. He imagined starting over and leaving his troubled past north of the border.

An 18-wheeler zoomed by, pushing a wall of air that rocked the Taurus. Harry opened his eyes and steered back onto the highway connecting him to every other in America. He tried to maintain his Mexican dream as he hit the gas, but the dream began to fade as he gained speed toward it, slipping like sand through his damaged fingers, until only the ache remained.

Chapter 4

Despite being born and raised in New York City, Dale Mayberry exuded an air of almost rural naïveté that some found endearing but most found unsettling in a man of his age and background. Equally unsettling was his inability to entirely mask the relentless ambition lurking beneath his apparent lack of guile.

The first political campaign Mayberry had ever managed delivered the 6th grade presidency to his classmate, Frank Nicoletti. That hard-earned victory had planted the seed that eventually grew into Mayberry's career. The competitive nature of the business rather than ideology or partisanship is what had attracted and drove him to work so hard at it. That and a candidate's ability to pay.

Though his record over the years had tallied far more "L's" than "W's," Mayberry's enthusiasm for campaign management had never wavered or waned. If anything, it had strengthened with each loss, the high number of which had inspired colleagues to dub him "Dale Defeat." Instead of wrecking Mayberry's self-esteem or tempering his confidence, the nickname actually had the opposite effect, fueling his desire to one day make the "Defeat" half of it pertain to his opponents rather than to himself.

He'd been closely following the Harry McBride story since it broke, having watched it so many times he even saw the punch projected against the backs of his eyelids when he tried to sleep at night; an increasingly difficult endeavor now that word of his incompetence had finally spread and job offers had slowed to a trickle. The anxiety this caused often kept Mayberry awake for hours, giving him plenty of time to review his professional and personal situations, to sort the pros and cons of each into markedly unequal piles. At least I don't have a wife and kids to support or a mortgage to pay, he'd remind himself, pleased that being single at age 41 and living solo in a Astoria, Queens one-bedroom walkup did have upsides.

He straightened and tightened his tie before entering the National Arts Club, on the south side of Gramercy Park.

"Here to meet Rex Tarsh," he told the doorman.

The doorman directed Mayberry up the white marble staircase. Mayberry turned right at the top and right again into a wood-paneled room decorated with old people and old furniture and somber-looking paintings. He spotted Rex Tarsh's silver hair above the back of a leather armchair occupying the French window overlooking the gated park.

"You beat me, Mr. Tarsh," he said, patting Tarsh's shoulder. "I always like to be first."

"This a meeting or a race?" Tarsh reached up and grasped Mayberry's hand extra firmly, the way a former athlete or former soldier might.

Mayberry sat in the armchair beside Tarsh's and looked out the window at a squirrel clawing its way up a tall, gnarled oak.

"Nice view."

Tarsh jabbed his thumb over his shoulder at two elderly women drinking tea.

"Nicer than looking at the corpses haunting this joint. Nag their husbands to death, then come here and plan how to spend their inheritance."

"They can always give some to me," Mayberry said, grinning.

"Course, my wife doesn't have to worry about inheritance. She did me the courtesy of dying first."

Mayberry exchanged his grin for an empathetic frown.

"My father told me. I'm sorry for your loss."

Tarsh waved it off.

"How's your dad, anyway? Haven't spoken to him in a while."

"He's thinking of retiring soon."

"Tell him retirement's not all it's cracked up to be."

"Why's that?"

"Next stop: the graveyard."

"I'd say you both have plenty of good years left."

Tarsh checked his watch, as if Mayberry had reminded him of precious time slipping away. He glanced at the portrait of a stodgy-looking man hanging on the wall beside him.

"My wife thought joining this place might instill some culture in me. Can't blame her for trying."

"It's a nice club."

"Nice and boring."

"Do you miss Wall Street?"

Tarsh shook his head.

"Me and my money are happy to sit on the sidelines now, watch everyone else jitterbug."

The mention of money had made Mayberry's stomach flutter.

"Can I get you a drink, Mr. Tarsh?"

"Not just yet. Get yourself one, if you want."

"No thanks. I'm what you'd call a teetotaler."

"Sorry to hear that."

"So, have you been following the Harry McBride story?"

It came out abruptly, skipping the smooth transition Mayberry had planned and hoped for.

"Some," Tarsh said, eyeing a pretty woman in a summer dress strolling through the park.

"What do you think?"

"The media these days'll milk crap like that for all it's worth."

"I couldn't agree more."

"They give people exactly what they want, which is to be angry, scared, and miserable."

"I believe it's the other way around. People want what they're given."

Tarsh transferred his attention from the woman to Mayberry.

"How do you mean?"

"I mean, when's the last time someone like Harry McBride's come along?"

Tarsh gestured to Gramercy, as if it represented the entire nation.

"America's full of morons like him."

"Harry McBride might be a moron, but he's also someone people can relate to. Not only because they sense he's one of them, but because of what he did."

"He slugged a senator and ran."

"Which is something *nearly every ordinary American would love to do if given half a chance and if they had the guts to.*"

Tarsh glanced at his watch.

"If this conversation were a movie, I'd say it doesn't have much plot."

"Okay, here it is: I want to start a grassroots organization based on Harry McBride. A society, so to speak, one that'll give average Americans something to believe in."

Tarsh narrowed his eyes at Mayberry, the way a lion sizing prey does.

"Let me ask you something, Dale. Have you gotten around to losing your virginity yet?"

"My *what*?"

"Have you ever been *laid*, son?"

Mayberry blushed.

"What kind of question is–Hey, I've been with plenty of women, Mr. Tarsh."

Tarsh smirked.

"Glad to hear it. Women tend to put things in perspective, keep fellas from becoming suicide bombers or video game addicts. So, let me get this straight: You want to start a grassroots something or other with Harry McBride, a man who happens to be a criminal and a fugitive."

"I want to start a grassroots *society*. And I don't want anything to do with Harry McBride, per se. I don't really need Harry McBride at all, just what he represents."

"Which is?"

"The reclaiming of America for the working class. Striking a blow for the have-nots way more directly than Barry Schwartz can. Leftie outlets like NPR are saying McBride represents direct, unambiguous opposition to decades of union busting and social safety net shredding and tax cutting for the rich while sending the poor to fight wars that protect corporate interests. For instance, you and my father fought in Vietnam to keep the price of Dupont Chemical stock up."

Tarsh glared at Mayberry.

"We fought for our *lives* boy."

"Point taken. I retract my last statement. But you get the idea."

Tarsh checked his watch again.

"I'm not exactly sure what your idea is. This is a capitalist country, in case you forgot."

"I'm well aware."

"Are you? Seems more like you've bought the malarkey that Schwartz guy is selling."

"You can't deny Schwartz might be onto something."

"Then why aren't you working for him?"

"I was going to," Mayberry lied. "We couldn't agree on terms."

Tarsh scrutinized the anonymous portrait again, then Mayberry, as if comparing the two men and finding the live one lacking.

"All right. You've given me a long-winded windup. What's the pitch?"

"I need capital to get this off the ground. I intend to raise it from different sources, but I'm giving you the opportunity to get in early and big because you're my father's friend."

"Who happens to have lots of dough."

"It'll be called the Harry McBride Society and it'll accept one-dollar donations from potentially every man, woman, and child in America. One dollar. No more, no less. To an organization that expresses their disgust with the rich and the powerful and the establishment. Just like Harry McBride did on that loading dock."

Tarsh began to tap his index finger against the armrest.

"You realize most of the people you'd be targeting would consider *me* one of the rich and the powerful and the establishment."

"Neither here nor there."

"Where the *hell* is it, then?"

Mayberry waited for Tarsh's irritation to settle.

"You'd be a silent partner, Mr. Tarsh. You see, whether he meant to or not, Schwartz begot McBride. And whether he meant to or not, McBride may have started a tidal wave we can both ride if we catch it right."

Tarsh looked down at his crotch.

"Harry McBride Society," he mumbled, seemingly to his balls.

"I can get it up and running relatively quickly. The webmaster from both Obama campaigns is pretty much onboard and he still has access to huge databases. I also have contacts at Crystal Wave, so I think we can put ads on their billboards all across the country. We could even stage fund-raising events in partnership with their radio stations within days."

"You mean while McBride's still on the run."

"It might be even better if he's caught and put on trial. Instant martyrdom, not to mention an extended news cycle. A portion of those donations could be used to pay his legal bills."

Tarsh shook his head slowly.

"Whole thing seems a bit far-fetched."

"Mr. Tarsh, as an investor you'd receive a percentage of every dollar that comes in, and I expect lots of them because we won't be asking anyone to make a big commitment or take any risk. We'll call them Rage Dollars or something like that. Each one a little Harry McBride punch thrown at the powers that be."

Tarsh twisted toward the bar on the other side of the room, then looked at Mayberry again.

"I'm still a little fuzzy. What exactly does this Harry McBride Society intend to accomplish with all this cash it collects from hacked-off Americans?"

"What it will do is give them a way to not only blow off steam, but to get the attention from their elected officials that the rich and the big corporations have been buying wholesale for years."

Tarsh gave Mayberry a skeptical look before glancing toward the bar again and pushing himself out of his chair.

"Wait a second."

Tarsh walked stiffly past the tea-drinkers and returned a minute later with a rocks glass of bourbon in one hand and a highball of seltzer in the other. He gave the seltzer to Mayberry who drank some, adding to the saliva now flooding his mouth.

"Tell me what you're thinking, Mr. Tarsh?"

Tarsh sat, dipped his pinky into his drink, and licked it.

"I'm thinking you might be like Thomas Edison."

"How's that?"

"The man finally succeeded by running out of ways to fail."

Mayberry ignored the slight.

"That mean you're in?"

"It means I never like to let a money-making opportunity pass without taking a good look. Money-making *is* what this is about, unless I'm missing something."

Mayberry smiled.

"There's no reason altruism can't be profitable, Mr. Tarsh."

Tarsh looked away from Mayberry, held up his glass, and peered through the bourbon at the amber-tinted park on the other side.

"No reason at all," he said before taking a sip.

Chapter 5

Kyle Baker stood in the doorway of Sargeant Gravel's break room and watched Mike Piccone, Pete McCall, and Bill Higgins play poker around an unsteady folding table. The three gravel workers studiously ignored their boss, adhering to the unwritten rule that gave Baker authority over them from 8:00am to 1:00pm and from 2:00pm to 5:00pm and permission to fuck off between 1:00pm and 2:00pm.

Baker cleared his throat.

"Listen up, guys. Someone here to talk to you."

This elicited neither a grunt nor a glance from Baker's three subordinates.

"He works for Senator Landon," he added.

Dragline operator Piccone chomped his baloney sandwich and exchanged a card.

"You mean Senator *Landed On His Ass?*"

Loader operator Higgins drank some Pepsi and burped into his fist.

"I swear I'll go insane if I don't get laid soon."

"It's known as Deadly Sperm Buildup," McCall, master of the gravel crushers, explained. "What you have, my man, is the old DSB."

"You're married, Higgins," Baker said. "What's the problem?"

Higgins gave his boss the same look he'd give a two-headed space alien. The three poker players resumed their game until Baker rapped his knuckles against the door jam.

"Hate to interrupt your little coffee klatch, fellas, but you have to talk to the man. Mr. Sargeant's orders. You first, Piccone."

Piccone waved his cards like a Japanese fan.

"C'mon, Kyle, I got a–"

"I don't care if it's a straight flush with ice cream and a cherry on top. He's in my office. Please don't steal anything while you're there."

Piccone threw down his cards and took another bite of sandwich.

"Don't tell him nothing," McCall coached.

Piccone stood and left the break room with a scowl. He ambled past the crushers to Baker's cramped and cluttered office, where he found Calvin Evans sitting behind Baker's desk with an officious smile on his face.

"Michael M. Piccone?"

Piccone gave the PI his weakest possible handshake.

"That's right."

"Please sit. I'm Calvin Evans. I've been hired by Senator Landon to ask some questions about Harry McBride and what happened here."

"I'm sure you saw it on TV like everyone else."

"I did, so there's not much about the actual assault I need. I'm more interested in Harry McBride the man, the one you've worked with for years."

"Thanks for clarifying."

"I understand you gambled with him on a regular basis."

"I wouldn't consider lunchtime poker gambling."

"No?"

Piccone grinned.

"Not when playing against Harry."

"You're saying he was an easy mark."

"I'm saying he was easy to win money from?"

"Why's that?"

"Too impulsive."

"No surprise. Do you think losing money might have put Harry under financial and perhaps emotional stress?"

Piccone lifted and inspected Baker's "World's Greatest Dad" trophy.

"We're just nickel and dime here, mister. Nothin' serious."

"Stress that may have prompted him to lash out?"

Piccone put down the trophy and looked at Evans.

"What I mean is we play for small stakes. Not enough to break anyone."

Evans noted that on his pad.

"If you don't mind me correcting something you just said, poker is, in truth, gambling, which, by definition, is the pursuit of unearned wealth and riches. Not good. But that's neither here nor there regarding my purposes today."

Piccone's eyed Evans suspiciously.

"I have no idea what the hell your purposes even are. Between Landon and you and the feds and the cops and all these goddamned reporters, I can't seem to enjoy my lunch hour in peace anymore."

Evans issued a slightly less officious smile.

"I apologize for the inconvenience, Mr. Piccone. Tell me, is Harry McBride what you'd call a disturbed individual? I ask because knowing his mental state could help me determine where he might have run to."

"Everyone here's a disturbed individual," Piccone said. "You work at a gravel plant twenty odd years, you'd be one, too."

"Have you ever noticed any signs of mental illness in Harry?"

Piccone splayed his hands.

"What do I look like, a psychiatrist?"

"Fair point. Before Harry attacked Senator Landon, did he ever act violently in any way?"

"I seen him stomp more than a few cockroaches over the years. He seemed to get a kick out of that."

"Any victims besides roaches? Any other instances like the one involving Landon?"

Piccone thought for a moment.

"He nearly went postal on me the time I ate half his sandwich. I was just trying to get his goat."

"His goat?"

"Bust his balls. That's what we do here. We bust rocks and balls."

"I see. What about his personal life?"

"What about it?"

"You tell *me*."

"We don't get all personal here."

"Women?"

"I like them. How about you?"

Evans tried to stone-stare the wiseass out of Piccone.

"I'm asking if there are any women in Harry's life."

"Not since Grace kicked him out."

"Grace, his wife?"

"Not anymore."

"Do you know why she kicked him out?"

"For being a depressed loser, I guess."

Evans wrote that Harry may be suffering from depression.

"Mr. Piccone, I want you to think before answering this. Did Harry do anything on a regular basis that struck you as strange? Any odd traits or habits?"

Piccone didn't reply at first; he seemed to be mulling something.

"Nope," he said, finally, defiance hardening his eyes. "He was just one of the guys. I guess he's a *celebrity* now."

"Suspect, not celebrity."

"Either way, he's still a knucklehead."

"So, where did this *knucklehead* go after assaulting Senator Landon?"

Piccone's body stiffened and he pulled back his head as if avoiding a punch.

"What are you sayin'? That I'm covering for him?"

"I said no such thing. But you've worked with him for years, so you may have some idea where he'd run to or hide."

Piccone's folded his arms across his chest.

"I got no clue."

"I find that hard to believe."

"Like I said, we don't get all personal here."

Piccone's cell phone rang then.

"Let whoever it is leave a message, please," Evans said. "That reminds me. Do you mind telling me which wireless provider you use? I ask because my AT&T service is sketchy here."

"Verizon's the only one that works at Sargeant," Piccone said. "Maybe because of the heavy machinery."

"Verizon, huh." Evans stood and reached across Baker's desk. "Thanks for your insights, Mr. Piccone. You've been very helpful."

Piccone gripped Evans's hand more firmly this time.

"Harry's a good guy, Mr. Evans. He don't have a mean bone in his body when it comes right down to it."

"I'll take that into consideration."

"Oh, he's a schmuck, don't get me wrong, but he's one of ours, so go easy on him."

"I'll do my best, Mr. Piccone."

"Want me to send in McCall or Higgins?"

"McCall or Higgins?"

"The idiots I play poker, I mean *gamble*, with. Don't you want to interrogate them, too?"

"No, I think I've gotten all I need. Thanks again."

Evans stopped in the waiting area on his way out of Sargeant; the wood-paneled, shag-carpeted room a relic from the mid-Seventies. Sally Durham's doe eyes cleared the speckled linoleum reception counter by only an inch or two.

"Anything I can help you with, Mr. Evans?"

Evans stepped closer to get a better look at the young receptionist, at her straight brown hair and trim body sheathed in a form-fitting sweater. Neither too much to handle nor too little to arouse, Evans thought. Most importantly, her girlish breasts registered on the smallish end of the normal male appreciation spectrum.

"I don't think there's anything more you could possibly do," Evans said. "It's Sally, correct?"

"You have a good memory."

"I do for certain things."

"You have a nice evening, Mr. Evans."

Evans bowed awkwardly.

"You as well, Sally."

Sally's smile waned as Evans and his smile lingered.

"Is there anything else you need?"

"Actually, just a follow-up to something I asked Mr. Piccone. Can you please tell me which wireless service you use?"

"I use Verizon."

"Verizon. I see. Much appreciated." Another idea came to Evans now that he'd confirmed which wireless provider McBride likely subscribed to. "One more request, Sally. Can you do me a ginormous favor and call my cell phone from yours? I've been having trouble receiving calls from other cell phones at this location. It's 203-756-9842."

Sally dialed the number and Evans answered.

"Hello, this is Calvin Evans," he said with a wink. "To whom am I speaking?"

"This is Sally Durham," the receptionist said, playing along.

"You mean the beautiful, charming, and *young* Sally Durham?"

Sally's face tensed slightly.

"That's me."

"Indeed, it is," Evans said. "And this, m'lady, is *moi*," he added, spreading his arms in the manner of a Broadway actor concluding a show tune.

Evans instantly reddened after underscoring his ridiculous modern English/Elizabethan English/French hybrid sentence with the equally ridiculous arm gesture. He quickly excused himself, chased from the waiting room by a mixture of embarrassment and shame. Though neither embarrassment nor shame prevented him from checking the "Recent Calls" log of his phone once he reached his minivan. *There it is!* Sally Durham's number, just begging to be dialed if timing and circumstance ever colluded with another lapse in his beleaguered willpower.

He drove aimlessly after leaving Sargeant, until he spotted the symbol of his favorite eating establishment ahead. His stomach panged as he approached the golden arches, a Pavlovian reaction almost completely divorced from true hunger. He parked beside the McDonalds and got out, yet something unseen, almost gravitational, compelled him to stop and turn before he reached the entrance of the fast food restaurant. That something happened to be Midnight Passion, one of the few porn shops the internet had failed to shutter. It stood like a siren directly across the road, the red neon sign above its doorway instantly captivating the PI, making him forget all about Big Macs and fries and Coke.

The sun had long since fled by the time Evans finally escaped Midnight Passion, his legs wobbly from his efforts inside. And though his stomach felt empty and his head felt light, his spirit rested like deadweight upon his shoulders.

"Take me to the river, Lord, to where Your righteous waters can douse my fires and cleanse my weak, pitiful soul."

Coincidence and luck rather than the Lord guided Evans from McDonalds to the deserted Hackettstown Riverfront Park. He parked and walked through darkness across a field of weeds and feral grasses that extended to the Musconetcong River. He stripped to his underpants at river's edge and waded in, stepping gingerly over slimy rocks until he lost his footing mid-stream and became baptized in stagnant water infused with mud and algae and industrial waste. He surfaced quickly, his "*Hallelujah!*" echoing off the maples lining the far bank.

He emerged from the river and stood on its narrow beach, the humid, breezeless New Jersey air struggling to dry him. He dressed still damp and returned to his car, his spirit mostly free of the burden it had carried out of Midnight Passion. He took his phone from his pocket and considered calling Sally Durham to see if she might join him for coffee. He resisted the urge and called Josh Weinberg instead.

"Joshua, it's Calvin Evans. How goes it?"

"Fair to middling," Josh said in his usual monotone. *"And you?"*

"You know the story of Job?"

"Got swallowed by the whale."

"Different guy. Anyway, how's Verizon treating you?"

"Like garbage, but I don't take it personally."

"We should both be thankful just to have jobs."

"Theoretically."

"Listen, I need help regarding someone who might be one of your customers. Harold S. McBride, from Hackettstown, New Jersey. Ever heard of him?"

"Who hasn't?"

"Our standard deal?"

"I could go to jail for divulging customer information."

"We've been through this before, Josh."

"Let's go through it again."

"Think of it as serving a higher cause. You Jews believe in that sort of thing."

"Not this Jew."

"Two hundred each time?"

"It's a federal offense, Evans. Plus, the FBI and Justice Department probably subpoenaed this shit already."

"Those numbskulls wouldn't know what to do with it. How about two fifty?"

"Make it three."

"*Three?* All right. But that's all I'm paying."

"I'll let you know where McBride is if he's dumb enough to make a call or send a text. You just PayPal me the money and don't jerk me around this time."

"You're an easy man to do business with, Josh."

"Sometimes I think I'm too easy."

Weinberg hung up and Evans started his car, confident he'd now be able to track Harry McBride if he happened to use his cell phone. He decided to formulate a Plan B just in case McBride either wasn't a Verizon customer or turned out to be savvier than he looked.

He looked up.

"Any ideas, Lord?...Gas stations? True, true. He *will* have to refuel every so often." He kissed his fingertips and touched the minivan ceiling. "'And forgive us our sins, for we also forgive everyone who is indebted to us. And do not lead us into temptation, but deliver us from the evil one.' Luke 11:4. But You already knew that, didn't You?"

Chapter 6

Shelbyville, TN (Day 7)

Harry had used a quarter to remove the license plates from the Taurus he'd been driving. He'd dropped the plates into a storm drain on a shaded side street in Roxboro, North Carolina, then replaced them with ones attached to a Chrysler Le Baron parked nearby. He'd substituted the Le Baron's plates with those belonging to a Honda Accord in a town called Hurdle Mills, a few miles away, hoping the double-switch would help him elude pursuers and buy time.

He'd driven all night from Hurdle Mills, parking just before dawn beside a small, weedy playground on the edge of Waynesville. Sleeping in the back seat at the playground had proved difficult; humidity and mosquitoes and dreams of Grace had kept it fitful and shallow, the rising sun and heat eventually yanking him from the embrace of their Catskill honeymoon. That magical week in the mountains followed him from his slumber and danced cruelly before his bleary eyes, the sex and laughter and long-gone ease taunting him the way memories of good things lost always did.

He sat up and looked out at the beech trees corralling the playground, the cicadas hidden in them singing louder as the temperature climbed. He left the car and peed on a patch of dead dandelions and watched the cottony seeds his stream freed drift away while he ran his fingertips over his shaved head and cheeks. Both still felt like they belonged to someone else.

He zipped up and retrieved from the glove compartment the peanut butter sandwich he'd made the night before. He brought it over to the swings and ate while sitting on the middle one, the tepid Poland Spring water he drank after each bite quenching his thirst but not his schoolyard memories of having to eat peanut butter while the other kids ate the ham and roast beef and turkey his mother could no longer afford after his father left.

Harry finished the sandwich and set the swing in motion by pushing his heels against the ground and pulling on the rusted chains. He did this until he'd swooped nearly as high as the cross bar. As a boy, he'd let go at this apex and savor the brief, weightless moments before his inevitable thud back to earth. He allowed the swing to slow to a stop instead of jumping.

"I used to swing 'til I was free. That was then. Now this is me."

He decided to write that down later if he could remember it. Now get back on the road, he told himself, before whoever's chasing catches up.

He drove the rest of the day after leaving Waynesville, the sign welcoming him to Tennessee from North Carolina the only indication that one state had ended and another had begun. The radio surfed mainly static until the scanner stopped and clarified on none other than Grover Budd.

"…where do you think our so-called president's true sympathies lie, having lived his formative years in a culture at war with

our own? Take a wild guess, Americans. But the more pressing question is where's Harry McBride? His wasn't just a crime against Senator Landon, it was a crime against our entire nation! It's called treason, for which a death sentence is not out of the question. So, you better run, Harry. You better hide. The gallows await. MUAH!!! Call me, McBride. 1-800-757-2900..."

Harry felt tempted to call Budd despite not knowing what he'd say to him. He felt an even stronger urge to punch the man, make the one he'd given Landon seem like a love tap in comparison. He turned off the radio and raised the windows, hoping to insulate himself from the world and what he'd done. He'd nearly succeeded until an overpass spray-painted *GO, HARRY, GO!* rushed toward then over him.

"What the fuck!"

The next overpass sported the same encouragement.

So did the one after it, but in different handwriting and in red rather than black paint.

"What kind of assholes would do something like that?" Harry asked himself, firmly back in reality now.

Route 70 took him to Murfreesboro, Tennessee. He followed Route 10 south from there and eased off the road into a fallow meadow just north of Shelbyville. He napped for an hour amongst tall, wheat-like grass and continued on as the sun dipped toward purplish mountains in the distance. Like the other towns he's driven through, little of Shelbyville's past remained to fight the franchise invasion. A small wooden structure marked by a simple "Uncle Sonny's BBQ" sign proved to be an exception.

Stick to peanut butter, Harry.

"You know I hate that shit, Grace."

Someone'll recognize you if you keep stopping at restaurants.

"I'll puke if I eat any more peanut butter."

You're wasting money, too.

Harry passed Uncle Sonny's and kept going until his appetite regained the upper hand, forcing him to pull off Route 10 and U-turn on Collier Avenue a mile later. He returned to Uncle Sonny's, parked in back, and donned his cap before entering.

"Here to eat?" asked the pretty yet sullen-looking woman at the door.

"Just beer," Harry mumbled, avoiding eye contact.

He pulled his cap lower and went to the bar, crowded with regulars and manned by a tall, shapeless bartender whose two-day growth couldn't hide a weak chin. Wooden picnic tables furnished the dining area, and a cook in whites stained by BBQ sauce occupied the cramped, open kitchen. Sweat coated the cook's face as he tonged baby backs from the smoker and cleaver-ed them with the dispassion of an executioner.

Harry ordered a bottle of Dixie lager and managed to ignore the TV, but only until Joe Landon appeared on it minutes later. The senator sat in a wheelchair outside St. Barnabas Medical Center, surrounded by reporters.

"Senator, you've been talking a lot about prayer since the assault," a reporter holding a Channel 5 microphone asked. *"Did you manage to pray here in the hospital this morning?"*

Landon's mouth tightened into a smile visible just below his mask.

"Of course, I did. I pray every day regardless of where I am and regardless of circumstance."

Landon cupped his hand behind his ear to better hear another question.

"*The subject of my prayers?*" he repeated. "*To be honest, I prayed for Harry McBride.*"

"*You prayed for the man who attacked you?*"

"*I prayed for God to save and redeem him.*"

"Good luck," Harry muttered.

Landon looked into the camera as if addressing Harry directly.

"*America's the land of second chances,*" he said. "*Pilgrims braved the oceans for one. So did the folks who ventured west from the east coast. Waves of European immigrants in the seventeen and nineteen hundreds came here yearning to breathe free and make a new start. I encourage Harry McBride to turn himself in so he can do the same.*"

Harry sensed a trap.

"*You mentioned immigrants, senator,*" a CNN reporter said. "*Can you explain your immigration policy?*"

Landon cleared his throat.

"*Despite what I just said about that, I think we can all agree immigration's a big problem. And I, um, I believe the only way to deal with it effectively is to increase border security, which means building the big wall all the way across our southern border.*"

What the fuck have immigrants ever done to you? Harry thought.

"*To be clear, businesses hiring the cheapest labor possible is how capitalism does and should work,*" Landon continued. "*That said, folks who sneak across our borders to steal American jobs are law breakers, plain and simple. Speaking of law breakers, I know the brave men and women of the Border Patrol are keeping an eye out for Harry McBride so he can be brought to justice.*"

"*But didn't you tell us you've been praying for Harry?*" another reporter asked.

Good question, Harry thought.

Landon's lips tightened into another smile. This one resembled a grimace.

"Mr. McBride's redemption can only begin after he's been arrested and he pays for what he's done. You have to clean a wound before it can heal, and we have to be consistent. I mean, if we're against illegal Mexicans flowing into our country, we can't allow illegal Americans, such as Harry McBride, to flow out of it."

We'll see about that, Harry thought.

He summoned the bartender and ordered smoked chicken wings, brisket, and a side of potato salad. He'd drained his beer by the time the food arrived, so he ordered another. Within minutes, only bones and two empties remained. Harry asked for a third Dixie and finally began to relax while drinking it. He recalled how the first two or three would relax his mother, too, but only until the next few pried open the door to her despair. Each night young Harry would watch Maureen McBride disappear through that door leading to the dark place where she'd hide from the world and from herself, until alcohol teamed with exhaustion to knock her into the next day.

The six o'clock news followed Landon's press conference, the top story featuring a full-screen of Harry's Sargeant employee ID photo. Harry listened more closely and learned that he remained at large and should be considered dangerous and possibly armed. The broadcast cut to a reporter outside Sargent describing Harry's tattoo as a cross between a Pegasus and a Unicorn. The next cut went to an enlarged still from the infamous punch footage–a grainy close-up of the actual tattoo illustrating Harry's right forearm.

"Nice tat," someone down the bar said.

The punch followed and Harry looked away just before Landon toppled off the loading dock. He ordered another

Dixie and a shot of Jack Daniels, hoping to rebuild the tenuous ease the news had destroyed. Alcohol rarely worked for long anymore, though a certain amount often moved his younger brother from the rear to the fore of his consciousness.

Harry had taken over as little Sean's father once their real one had left for good, a role that had suited him more easily and naturally than any other. The thought of Sean toddling down the upstairs hallway, his bunchy diapers swaying from side to side, brought a smile to Harry's lips as he sat there at Uncle Sonny's bar. He imagined he'd call Sean right now if things had turned out differently.

The Tennessee whiskey had joined with the beer to spread fumy warmth through his body. He caught the bartender's eye and pointed to his empty shot glass. The refill slid down his throat and put Sean on the barstool beside him.

Look at you, big brother. A real hero.

Harry laughed quietly.

"That's Mr. Hero to you, pal."

Where you headed, Harry?

"Mexico."

Just don't drink the water.

"Only cerveza and tequila for me."

Not a bad punch you threw. I coulda done better.

"You couldn't punch your way out of a paper bag, little man."

I never needed to. You always did it for me.

A knot of grief tightened the base of Harry's throat.

"I'm still punching for ya, kid."

Maybe it's time you stop.

Harry drank more beer and shook his head.

"I shoulda done a better job."

I'm the one who should have done better.

Harry resisted the urge to bury his face in his hands so he could cry without drawing attention.

"Come with me, Sean."

I can't.

"Why not?"

Because I'm dead, Harry.

Harry recalled that awful morning; Sean cold and stiff in his bed, a dose of bad heroin filling his veins. The fifteen years since then seemed to have passed in a blink and an eternity.

"I know you are," he said.

He looked down and wished he could climb into his shot glass and stay there. He sensed Sean still on the stool beside him, a shadowy presence teasing the corner of his vision. He didn't dare turn and look directly at his brother, fearful he might disappear again or, even worse, become just another stranger.

Uncle Sonny's had emptied while the booze had taken Harry on its ride. The room had begun to spin when he'd closed his eyes, forcing him to grab the lip of the bar. He found the woman who'd greeted him at the door sitting beside him when he opened his eyes again, her lips curled into a semi-smile, her manicured fingers gripping a sweating Dixie bottle. Harry blinked her into focus and wondered if she'd once been a cheerleader or a prom queen.

"I'm Lucinda," she said in a soft, mid-south accent.

Harry took her hand in his and held it an extra moment or two before releasing it.

"I'm Maxwell. Nice to meetya."

"Where you from, Maxwell?"

"Me? From all over."

"A real rambling man."

"I get around."

"Do you happen to have a last name, *Maxwell?*"

"A last name? Sure, I got one."

Lucinda gave Harry a bemused smile.

"Care to tell me?"

Harry hesitated while racking his brain.

"It's, uh…it's Shelby," he said, unable to think of anything else.

Lucinda's smile became a smirk.

"Shelby, huh? This happens to be Shelbyville, you know."

"What are the chances of that?"

Lucinda's eyes dropped to Harry's forearm, exposed by the sleeve he'd rolled at some point.

"About as slim as you having the exact same horse thingy tattoo as a man named Harry McBride."

Harry would have panicked had he been sober.

"You're a sharp one," he said.

"I keep my eyes open."

"What'll take to close 'em?"

Weak, pre-dawn light seeped through a thin, once-white curtain, allowing Harry to see Lucinda's wedding band for the first time.

"You're married," he said, his voice thick from the alcohol he'd consumed the night before.

Lucinda's sigh seemed one with the sad little motel room. She handed Harry a glass of still-cloudy water she'd drawn from the bathroom sink.

"I am...to Sonny."

"Where was Sonny last night?"

"Behind the bar." Lucinda yawned into her fist. "He figures letting me do this once in a while's cheaper than alimony
and losing half his restaurant, if you can call it that."

Harry pressed his palm to his throbbing forehead and
drank some water.

"How'd we get here?"

"I drove. You were in no shape."

"I hope I was in shape for *something*."

"You're not my type, but you do have a kind of primal
caveman thing going on."

"Thanks...I guess."

Harry noticed his clothes strewn across the worn green
carpet, and wondered how quickly he could get into them and
out the door.

"You were in Uncle Sonny's last night for a reason," Lucinda said.

"The reason is I was tired of driving and eating peanut
butter and I needed a cold one real bad."

Lucinda took the glass from Harry and drank, leaving a
faint lipstick mark on the rim.

"I'm coming with you."

Harry sat up and the pain flowed from his forehead to
his temples.

"You can't come with me."

"Why not?"

"'Cause I'm an outlaw."

"So?"

"And a fugitive."

Lucinda smiled, almost wistfully.

"We'll be like Bonnie and Clyde."

Harry detected no signs of insanity in her eyes, only determination, which he found even more worrisome.

"Your life here that bad?"

"I hate my husband."

"Most women hate their husbands."

"Most women hate *my* husband."

"What about kids?"

"Michael's sixteen and Hannah's fourteen and a half, so they're almost legal."

"You'd leave your family just like that?"

"I'm bored, Harry."

"You'd be even more bored in jail. Aiding and abetting or something."

Lucinda seemed unfazed.

"You know that song, I Hope You Dance? The one from years ago about taking chances in life?"

"I mostly listen to the Stones and Springsteen. Look, you already got what you wanted from me."

Lucinda suddenly wrapped her arms around Harry's neck and pressed her face into him.

"I was born in Shelbyville," she said, her words muffled by Harry's chest. "I was raised here, got married here, had two kids here." She pulled away. "I damned sure ain't gonna die here. Thirty-four years in Shelbyville, Tennessee's enough."

"What if I don't take you?"

"Then I'll just call my friends in the Shelbyville Police Department. I'll do it, too."

"I don't doubt it."

"Think of the fun we'd have."

Harry grabbed her shoulders and shook her gently.

"Wanna know why I hit that senator? Because I'm crazy."

Lucinda's eyes had lost focus, as if she'd already left Shelbyville far behind.

"No, you're not."

Harry's headache sharpened along with his sense of impending doom.

"Listen to me. I'm a fucked-up New Jersey gravel worker. That's all I am and all I'll ever be. My wife left me and my back always hurts and I'm depressed most of the time. I can't control myself very well, either. You saw that."

"We all have our issues, honey." Lucinda's accent sounded even more southern now. "Take me away from all this."

She reclined and arced her bare breasts toward the low ceiling. Harry couldn't deny she looked good in that position, and the battle against his resurgent desire proved to be a brief and losing one.

"We'll rest a while before going," he said afterward, his heart and lungs laboring from his efforts.

"Rest." Lucinda nestled her head into the hollow dividing Harry's chest from his right shoulder. "Good idea."

"Don't want you tired out there on the road."

"Can't be tired," Lucinda murmured, already fading.

Harry waited until her breath had settled before carefully sliding out from beneath her. He rolled off the bed and dressed quickly and quietly, nerves and adrenaline temporarily easing his hangover. Shelbyville can't be so bad, he thought, looking down at the sleeping woman. Can't be much worse than Hackettstown or anywhere else.

He made sure Lucinda remained unconscious before going over to the table beneath the window and taking her phone and car keys from her bag. He slid them into his pocket, then opened her purse and removed the $86 from it. He tiptoed to the door with the money, but stopped instead of opening it; paralyzed by a sudden sadness that stayed general at first before focusing on Lucinda. The thought of her so desperate to escape her life is what had plunged Harry into a despondence that threatened to trap him in the motel room. Nearly a minute passed before he managed to break its grip and return to the table.

You're a stupid man, he told himself as he slipped the $86 back into the purse.

He then left the room with Lucinda's keys and phone, hoping that would give him enough of a head start. He crossed the parking lot to the empty highway and turned toward Uncle Sonny's, his vision and thoughts still skewed by the beer and whiskey he'd drank there, his head pounding even worse now.

Chapter 7

Martin "Papa Marty" Reynolds strode across the stage, pretending to be on some kind of mission. He faced the crowd when he reached the center and threw a punch into the hot, late summer air. The throng filling the Batesville, Mississippi Piggly Wiggly parking lot surrounding the stage issued a loud *"YEAH!"* and threw a collective punch right back at the WKPU morning DJ. Dale Mayberry, standing at the edge of the gathering, punched along with them.

Reynolds pulled a microphone from his back pocket and brought it to his lips.

"Awright! Awright! Awright! You guys sure can *swing!*"

HELL YEAH!

"But what are we *really* here for?" Reynolds said, gesturing to the giant American flag draped over the front of the stage.

AMERICA!

"Damned straight! And every dime we raise at the WKPU Harry McBride Punch-Out Contest today is going to the Republican National Committee. The good, old RNC. The only organization still willing and able to make America rock and roll again!"

ROCK AND ROLL! ROCK AND ROLL!

"You know what else? We're gonna help the good ol' US of A throw its *own* Harry McBride punch!"

U-S-A! U-S-A! U-S-A!

Reynolds gauged the spectators sweltering beneath the blazing sun and wondered how many were gathered this morning at similar Harry McBride Punch-Out Contests organized by the Harry McBride Society and sponsored by Crystal Wave radio stations across the nation. He hoped this one had sold enough tickets to raise the $30,000 minimum his special event bonus required.

A liberal product of the Sixties, Reynolds had nearly quit the day right-wing Crystal Wave bought independent WKPU fifteen years ago. Working for the embodiment of everything he despised had seemed unthinkable to Reynolds at the time. But not as much as shirking his financial responsibilities or spitting in the face of a tight DJ job market. So, he'd swallowed his pride and stayed on, somehow managing to grin while bearing it.

The crowd entertaining itself with *"U-S-A! U-S-A! U-S-A!"* gave Reynolds the chance to drift back nearly four decades, to the dead man's shift he'd once worked as a student DJ at the University of Mississippi radio station. Best gig he'd ever had; playing whatever he'd wanted to, not caring that few stayed up late enough to hear deep cuts from Depeche Mode's new album or his impassioned diatribes against U.S. foreign policy in Central America. The bout of nostalgia brought tears to his eyes that went unnoticed by the sweaty mass assembled at the foot of the stage, its singular voice braying unwavering conviction, its array of indistinguishable faces free of any discernable doubts.

Reynolds blinked back his tears as their fists flew toward him and their *"U-S-A! U-S-A! U-S-A!"* assaulted his ears. He thought of Jesus bestowing compassion and forgiveness on those who'd cheered His crucifixion and wished he could do the same for this deluded mob. Even amoebas know their enemies, he thought. These creatures clearly don't.

He brought the microphone to his lips again.

"You guys are great! You're the true Americans who care about our heritage and our way of life and our *freedom!*

WOO-HOO!

I know its hotter'n Georgia blacktop in August. Hang on a minute! This is *Mississippi* blacktop in August! Which is even hotter! But y'all came despite the heat and y'all seem anxious to get started! So let's *do it!*"

WOO-HOO!

Reynolds turned toward a pot-bellied man standing on the right side of the stage, a fake beard and shoulder-length wig making him look much like Harry McBride had when he'd hit Landon.

"Ladies and gentlemen, our first 'Harry McBride' comes from just down the road, in Courtland!"

HAR-RY MC-BRIDE! HAR-RY MC-BRIDE! HAR-RY MC-BRIDE!

Reynolds approached the contestant, who wore a black t-shirt with a hand-painted *"POW!"* emblazoned across the chest. "Morning, sir. How ya doing?"

"I'm doing just great, Papa Marty."

"That's good. Have you signed the waiver?"

"Yes, I have, Papa Marty."

"Did you happen to read it before you signed?"

"I'm here to help the country," the man said. "I'm here because of 9-11 and ISIS and Muslim terrorists and all that, not to read a bunch of small lawyer writing."

"What about the Mexicans?" a woman shouted from the crowd.

"I'm here 'cause of them, too!"

> *BUILD THE WALL! BUILD THE*
> *WALL! BUILD THE WALL!*

"Awright, then," Reynolds said once the chant had died down. "You're all set."

He walked to the other side of the stage, occupied by a man in an ill-fitting, thrift store suit.

"Everyone, let's give it up for our first 'Joe Landon' of the day!"

"Lan-don! Lan-don! Lan-don!" someone called out in sing-songy cadence.

> *LAN-DON! LAN-DON! LAN-DON!*

Reynolds held up his hand for quiet.

"Have you signed the waiver, Senator Landon?"

"I have."

"And did *you* happen to read it first?"

"Yes, I did."

"Excellent. Since Harry McBride over there explained why he's participating in the contest, I'll give you the same opportunity."

The contestant representing Senator Landon took the microphone from Reynolds.

"I'm here because America's the greatest country in the world and each and every American has to fight for it, even if that means taking a beating once in a while. *So bring it on!*"

BRING IT ON! BRING IT ON! BRING IT ON!

Reynolds reclaimed the microphone.

"There you have it, folks. A man willing to *'take a beating'* for his country!"

TAKE A BEAT-ING! TAKE A BEAT-ING!
TAKE A BEAT-ING!

Reynolds became more spectator than host from then on, watching as if from above while his Papa Marty alter ego ushered one after another "McBride" and "Landon" into position, then stepped back as each "McBride" punched each "Landon" in the face. He cringed inwardly whenever a fist unhinged a jaw or blood spurted from a flattened nose or a voluntary victim issued an involuntary scream. One man stiffened like a board after being punched, unconscious even before hitting the stage with a sickening whump. The crowd's roar of approval after each assault sounded like crashing waves to Reynolds, intervals of relative calm in between. But their faces, contorted by blood-lust glee, are what alarmed him most. Where does it come from? he wondered. Where will it ultimately go?

He talked his talk the entire time, desperately pretending to actually believe and not be horrified by what he said. Yet his fallacious banter failed to obscure his deep fear of and contempt for these listeners who indirectly paid his salary, much of which went to his ex-wife these days. He felt ready to choke on his distain by the time the latest "McBride" punched the latest "Landon."

The blow landed solidly and hard enough to send "Landon" stumbling right into Reynolds. The collision knocked the unprepared DJ across the stage to its edge, where he teetered for several moments. The tarmac seemed to rush upward once Reynolds lost the remainder of his balance and fell off, the sharp, sudden impact jolting the microphone from his hand and the breath from his lungs.

The crowd quieted as Reynold lay stunned on his back, pain exploding through his body, angry sun rays stabbing into his eyes. Those rays were blocked moments later by Dale Mayberry, who Reynolds had met briefly before the event. Mayberry stood over the fallen DJ, the sun blasting from behind him obscuring the mild concern creasing his brow. He asked Reynolds if he was okay just as the crowd emerged from its hush.

PA-PA MAR-TY! PA-PA MAR-TY! PA-PA MAR-TY!

The chant acquired a taunting, menacing edge as it grew faster and louder:

PA-PA MAR-TY! PA-PA MAR-TY! PA-PA MAR-TY!

Reynolds remained prone, searching for the strength to answer Mayberry and for the will to rise and face his listeners again. Unable to find either, he closed his eyes and wished he could close his ears, too. Who am I to get up? he thought as the chant switched back to *BUILD THE WALL! BUILD THE WALL! BUILD THE WALL!* Who the fuck am I?

Chapter 8

Harry McBride crossed into a new day soon after crossing from Tennessee into Arkansas. The road began to swerve between the Ozarks, which looked like shadows against blue-black sky. The ancient hills reminded Harry of Sargeant gravel piles, also of giant waves he imagined surfing all the way to a big margarita beach somewhere south of the Rio Grande.

He switched on the radio to chase his drowsiness, and listened to a Grover Budd listener describe her late-night encounter with him outside a Worchester, Massachusetts truck stop. The woman bragged in a heavy New England accent of eliciting Harry McBride's soft, tender side. Budd told her Harry had no soft, tender side. He also told her Harry had reportedly been with a woman in Tennessee that very night, making her alleged tryst with him in Massachusetts unlikely, if not impossible. The woman insisted it *had* been Harry who'd gently ravished her in the back seat of her Honda, and that they now shared an unbreakable bond.

"You're both sluts!" Budd snapped. *"That's your bond!"*

Harry turned off the radio and followed Route 27 through a series of sleeping towns, none much more than a handful of modest homes clustered around a deserted intersection. He stopped at the light in one called Douglas Corner and looked into a living room infused with flickering blue. He saw a man watching TV with a remote control in hand and wondered if insomnia or anxiety or perhaps a loveless marriage had kept him awake.

The light changed and Harry drove off still thinking about the man, imagining him stranded in that house at that crossroad until death finally freed him.

Don't worry about him, Harry. You got your own problems.

"I'm not worried about him."

He reminds you of yourself, don't he?

"Enough of the psycho analyzation, Grace."

A neon sign ahead provided welcome distraction from Grace's imagined needling. The sign drew Harry to a place named Lakehouse Lounge, where he parked facing the street to allow quick escape. He got out and peeked through the ripped screen covering the tavern's front window. He saw only a bartender and two men shooting pool inside. "Sweet Melissa" flowed from the jukebox, a song that had always moved him.

He stood by the window, the song's nostalgic lyrics and melancholy chords taking him back to the hot, hollow summers of his New Jersey youth. He always remembered those days in black and white and beige no matter how hard he tried to paint them brighter. "Sweet Melissa" had been a hit back then, always invoking in Harry the image of an ethereal-looking girl with gentle eyes and winsome smile.

He remained at the window after the song ended, unsure if he should risk going in for a beer. He heard the pool players talking between songs.

"I'm telling ya, he goes all the way to Thailand to get laid," the bigger one said. "Twenty-seven hour flight just to get some pussy."

"He can't find any closer to home?" the smaller pool player said.

"Twenty-five bucks for a girl over there."

"For an hour?"

"For *a day*."

"No shit."

"They even do your laundry."

"Speaking of girls, we should head down to Venus."

"Naw, I'm trying to be good."

"You're trying to be a pussy is what you're trying to be."

The bigger player glared at the smaller one before moving to the other side of the table and lining his next shot. He crouched and looked beyond his stick to the cue ball, then beyond the cue ball to Harry, still at the window. The man's face remained blank at first before going slack-jawed with stunned recognition. He straightened slowly, as if to avoid scaring Harry off. But Harry had already bolted before the man had gotten fully upright, glad he'd parked his car facing out.

Chapter 9

Chris Watkins breezed into Senator Landon's office with a wry expression on his face.

"Lobbyists are massing in the lobby...as it were."

Landon returned from a brief mind trip to his Idaho boyhood.

"Bunch of locusts."

"Ones who don't realize you won't be able to feed them if you don't devote time to getting elected."

"Unfortunately, they're feeding *me* right now."

"Cyrus Peterson's first. Energy Producers Alliance."

"Those tightwads didn't give as much as I expected."

"Let him read Popular Mechanics a while longer?"

"Yeah. Take a seat."

Watkins sat in one of the chairs facing Landon's desk and stifled a laugh; the sight of his boss in a mask still tickled him.

"What's on your mind?"

"Any new thoughts on Harry McBride?"

Watkins shrugged.

"Either he's extremely crafty or law enforcement in this country's a bigger joke than I thought."

Landon let out a short breath.

"He should be inside a jail by now. Instead, he's allegedly been inside every antsy housewife from New Jersey to Tennessee."

"No accounting for taste."

Earl Tibbens knocked on the door jam, his weathered, late middle-aged face portraying just the right mixture of experience and gravitas, each line in it representing an all-American value.

"I've drafted the white paper detailing our education reform positions, Joe. Take a look?"

Nothing interested Joe less at the moment. Truth be told, his preferred education reform entailed scrapping the Department of Education altogether. He smiled tepidly at his running mate.

"When you're finished with it, Earl."

"Sounds good. Just wanted to keep you in the loop."

Landon felt relieved that Tibbens didn't dawdle. Few people bored him more.

"Harry McBride," Watkins said after Tibbens had left. "Polls say a majority of Americans hope he escapes."

"I don't have much faith in polls."

"Me neither. But most seem to say the same basic thing."

"Which is?"

"McBride's becoming quite popular."

"Ain't that something."

"Get this. Gallup asked people who they'd rather have a beer with: you or Harry McBride. Seventy-six percent said they'd rather have one with McBride."

"Why would anyone want to drink with that cretin?"

"A CNN/NY Times poll asked respondents whether they'd switch places with McBride if they could."

Landon put his hands over his mask and peeked through his fingers.

"Do I want to hear this?"

"Eighty-one percent said they would. My question is do you really want to lead a nation of such imbeciles?"

"I'm beginning to wonder."

"One more poll."

"Do you have to?"

"This is particularly telling. Quinnipiac asked over fifty thousand people who they'd prefer to be their president, Harry McBride or the man who currently holds the office."

"Thanks for not saying his name in here."

"Sixty-eight percent said they'd prefer …drum roll please… *Harry McBride*."

Landon rested his forehead in his palm, although he actually agreed with the respondents this time.

"Why would Quinnipiac waste time polling crap like that?"

"Good question." Watkins glanced at his watch. "Don't want to keep Peterson waiting too long."

He left the office and the lobbyist appeared a minute later.

"C'mon in, Cyrus," Landon said.

"Good to see you, Joe." Peterson shook Landon's hand and settled into the chair Watkins had warmed. "How you feeling?"

"Foolish, mainly."

"This thing's certainly given you lots of exposure."

"The kind I could do without."

"The whole victim compassionate forgiver approach is clever."

Landon jabbed his thumb into his chest.

"My idea."

"I'm impressed."

"Between you, me, and the walls, I don't actually have any compassion or forgiveness for McBride."

"I wouldn't, either."

"That's one thing we agree on. Where else can we find common ground?"

Peterson smiled, clearly glad to be done with niceties.

"Interesting you mention ground. Because the ground in parts of your state happens to contain a fair amount of oil and natural gas."

"'We're not just potatoes anymore' should be our new state motto."

"How about 'Idaho: Saudi Arabia of the Midwest'? Geologists say we're still just scratching the surface."

"And you're here today because the boys you represent want to scratch a little deeper."

"A *lot* deeper."

Landon sensed an opportunity to leverage a bigger campaign donation. His mind had also strayed to the poll figures Watkins had just cited, and beyond those figures to why he'd gotten into this business in the first place. It no longer seemed so clear.

"Obstacles," he said to Peterson. "Municipalities, environmentalists, state and federal agencies, to name a few."

"That's why we're talking, senator."

Landon decided to let Peterson twist in the wind a bit.

"Let me ask you something, Cyrus. What do you think Harry McBride's stance on the fossil fuel industry is?"

Peterson seemed confused.

"You're asking me Harry McBride's opinion on fossil fuels?"

"I mean, do you think he's supportive of them or do you think he's one of those wind-solar-geothermal power nuts?"

Peterson looked at Landon as if trying to see through his mask and determine if Harry had knocked the sense out of him.

"It wouldn't surprise me if he doesn't have any opinions at all on the subject."

Landon tented his fingers in front of his mouth.

"Which means he could probably be swayed one way or the other fairly easily."

"Why do you want to know, if you don't mind me asking?"

Landon shrugged.

"No reason. Nothing in particular. I suspect you're as busy as I am, so let's talk Idaho oil."

"And natural gas."

"That too."

Chapter 10

Calvin Evans lay atop the bedspread, afraid to turn it down and climb under. Because God only knew what lurked in these motel sheets; one shady patron after another indulging in all types of sordid acts between them. Evans conveniently ignored the fact that he himself had been one of those shady patrons when he'd taken the young girl to the Alexandria, Virginia Motel 6.

Still no word from Josh Weinberg at Verizon, which had forced Evans to rely on old-fashioned investigating. This included assessing the mainly dubious testimony of self-proclaimed Harry McBride witnesses. He hadn't bothered to follow up on the alleged Worchester, Massachusetts truck stop encounter he'd heard about on the Grover Budd Show, but the one involving a Tennessee woman named Lucinda Johnson had seemed plausible enough to lure him to this rundown Days Inn, in Murfreesboro, Tennessee.

He rested a few more minutes before showering and shaving and taking Route 231 thirty miles south to Shelbyville. He had no trouble finding Uncle Sonny's BBQ and Lucinda greeting customers at the door. He flashed his badge at her.

"Do you have a minute, ma'am?"

"I'm busy."

"So am I. Take a break."

They sat at an unoccupied table and Evans explained his connection to Senator Landon.

"I'm going to ask you direct questions and I'd like direct answers, Ms. Johnson."

"It's *Mrs.* Johnson. You can call me Lucinda."

"Okay, Lucinda. It'll start with what I ask everyone who claims to have encountered Harry McBride. How do you know it was him?"

Lucinda gave Evans an impatient look.

"How about he looked just like Harry McBride, he had the same stupid tattoo as Harry McBride, and he admitted to being Harry McBride when I called him out on it?"

"Seems you've covered your identification bases pretty well. Please don't take this the wrong way, but why did you sleep with him, *then* call the cops?"

Lucinda tensed.

"The answer to the first part of your question is none of your business."

"That a married woman chooses to commit adultery isn't my concern, I'll concede. How about the second part? You obviously liked Harry at one point. What changed your mind?"

Lucinda glanced over at Sonny behind the bar.

"He stole my car keys and phone, for one."

Evans wrote that down. The phone could possibly be tracked.

"You brought Harry back to the motel, slept with him, and he then stole your car keys and cell phone?"

"Didn't even have the decency to say goodbye."

"Oh, he's one of *those* guys."

Lucinda nodded.

"Gets to have his fun, then just hit the road."

"Life's not always fair."

"Tell me about it. He was off on his next adventure while I was doing the walk of shame all the way back here, in my high-heels, no less."

Evans softened his tone.

"I understand your frustration, Lucinda. Believe me, I do."

"I mean, I'm stuck in Shelbyville the rest of my life."

"Any idea where Harry might be headed?"

"He didn't exactly leave me his itinerary."

"Did he happen to talk about his route or plans in general at any point?"

Lucinda thought for a moment.

"He might have mentioned Mexico. Maybe I just read that. Either way, where else would he be going?"

"I've drawn the same conclusion."

"Then why are you asking me what you already know?"

"Good investigators don't assume anything or leave any stone unturned."

Lucinda gave Evans a coquettish smile.

"If Harry's going to Mexico, I guess that means you are, too."

Evans looked up from his note pad.

"To be honest, I hope to catch him before he gets there or even close. But if I have to follow him over the line, that's what I'll do."

Lucinda smiled at Evans, then leaned to within inches of his face.

"Take me with you," she said, looking straight into his eyes.

"Take you with me?"

"*Please* take me with you."

Exhausted from a day spent interviewing gas station and convenience store clerks, then Lucinda Johnson, Evans returned to the Murfreesboro Days Inn. He lay on the bed and tried his best to get inside Harry McBride's head, to imagine what had driven him to hit Landon and what his subsequent plan might be. He tried to imagine himself as Harry and decided the man wouldn't do anything too unusual or creative. Stick to the basics and you'll find him, Calvin.

He turned on the TV and watched the local news, comprised mostly of crimes committed in the Memphis metropolitan area. He paid scant attention to the broadcast until the story following the weather; it featured two locals who claimed to have been assaulted by Harry McBride in a nearby roadhouse. Evans sat up and jotted the location and names of the alleged victims. Tommy McCracken, the larger of the two, sported a swollen, lopsided jaw. Kevin Widner, the smaller, stockier man, had a metal splint taped to the bridge of his nose. Evans couldn't help snickering at their appearance.

He parked outside Lakehouse Lounge less than an hour later and opened his Bible to Galatians 6:9:

"And let us not grow weary while doing good, for in due season we shall reap if we do not lose heart."

He reread the passage before getting out of his minivan and entering the roadhouse. He found a spot near the end of the bar and ordered a club soda with lime.

"Say, you don't happen to know where I can find them two fellas that got clocked by Harry McBride last night?" Evans asked when the heavyset bartender delivered the lime-less soft drink.

The man jerked his chin toward McCracken and Widner, who stood by the pool table surrounded by several women and a couple of eager, envious-looking dudes.

"Get in line, if you wanna talk to 'em."

Evans sucked his teeth the way he'd seen white trash and ghetto blacks do it.

"Seems gettin' thrashed by ol' McBride kinda ups a man's popularity around here."

The bartender scoffed.

"Those losers think they're hot shit now, talking to cops and FBI and pretty girls. Just for getting beaten up."

"Better lucky than talented is what I say. Did you happen to witness the big event?"

"Alls I know is it didn't happen while I was here. You one of them reporters?"

"Let's just say I'm here at the behest of Senator Landon."

The bartender eyed Evans doubtfully.

"Why would Senator Landon *behest* the likes of you? That's two dollars for the club soda."

Evans laid three on the bar.

"By the way, you forgot the lime."

"You didn't ask for one."

"Oh, I did all right," Evans said, abandoning what remained of his folksy routine.

"No, you didn't."

Evans smiled stiffly.

"Perhaps you were so eager to serve me you didn't hear the second part of my order, which regarded the lime."

Evans felt sure one would plop into his glass now that he'd pointed out the omission. The bartender instead scooped

Evans's dollars, dropped all three into his tip cup, and wandered off.

Fuming from the lime battle loss, Evans moved away from the bar, past a guy playing video poker, a drunk sleeping with his head on a table, and an unattractive man snaking his tongue into an equally unattractive woman's mouth. He noticed a deer head mounted above the men's room door, a wrinkled cigarette wedged between its lips. Poor beast must have died of lung cancer, he thought before stopping beside the young woman fawning over Tommy McCracken.

"Excuse me, miss. Hate to interrupt, but I need a word with Mr. McCracken." He waved his PI badge at her. "Official business."

He turned to the man talking to Kevin Widner.

"You, too, sir, if you don't mind."

Evans faced McCracken and Widner once their admirers had left.

"Gentlemen, my name's Calvin Evans. I work for Senator Landon and I have some questions for you."

"We didn't do nothin' wrong," McCracken said.

"I'm not saying you did."

"We was the victims," Widner said. "Just like Landon."

"Clearly you were. I'm only here to confirm it was actually Harry McBride who did the victimizing."

McCracken's eyes began to shift a bit, like those of a cornered animal.

"It *was* Harry McBride."

"How do you know?"

"Because he said so."

"What exactly did this man claiming to be Harry McBride say?"

"He said, 'Don't fuck with Harry McBride.'"

Widner nodded.

"That's what he said just after he cleaned Tommy's clock and just *before* he cleaned mine."

Evans pretended to ponder the story, although it sounded a little too on the nose, so to speak.

"You know, whenever there's been a high-profile incident, such as Harry McBride attacking Senator Landon, similar ones often follow. They're called copycat crimes, sometimes committed by individuals trying to assume the original perpetrator's identity."

McCracken's eyes steadied as his decision to stick by his story entrenched.

"It was Harry McBride," he said. "Believe me."

"Did he look like McBride?"

"He had a shaved head and face. Other than that he looked the same as the guy on TV who punched Landon."

"And he threw straight rights," Widner added. "Same punch he hit Landon with."

"Most people are right-handed," Evans said. "Which means most would throw a straight right."

McCracken caressed his injured jaw.

"Look, mister, we *know* it was Harry McBride."

Evans had started to find the interview more amusing than useful.

"Assuming it actually had been McBride, why would he have attacked two perfectly nice, upstanding fellas such as yourselves? Did you say anything to provoke him? Did you bump into him or give him a dirty look?"

McCracken's eyes dilated with feigned innocence. *Give this man an Academy Award,* Evans thought.

"We didn't have nothing to do with him," McCracken said. "We was just playing pool and talking about whether to go to Venus after. Then I look out the window and see McBride staring in at me real mean like. I look right back at him and he apparently don't like that and in he comes."

"Hang on a minute," Evans said. "You mentioned Venus. Were you planning to fly your spaceship there?"

Widner seemed annoyed by Evans attempt at humor.

"Venus is the strip joint down the road. I wanted to go, but Tommy didn't want to. So, I called him a pussy and that's when Harry showed up."

Evan wrote *Widner wanted to go to strip joint. McCracken didn't. Possible fight between McCracken and Widner regarding evening plans.*

"Understood," he said, confident now that the two men had actually gotten into an argument, *punched each other*, then concocted the Harry McBride story to cover their embarrassment while also getting some of the attention they'd been craving their entire pathetic lives. He glanced at their knuckles and noticed they did look a bit red. "Please, go on."

"So, McBride comes in and goes at Tommy like a bat outta hell," Widner said.

Hell. Evans couldn't help smiling at the opportunity to make something out of this nothing burger.

"Tell me, have you guys ever considered that whoever assaulted you–Harry McBride or not–may have been possessed? A *demon* rather than the proverbial *bat* out of hell?"

The two friends traded perplexed looks.

"Surely you must know this drinking establishment is a nexus of sin," Evans said.

McCracken and Widner remained flummoxed; Evans forged ahead.

"I don't know if either of you attend church, but you'll never encounter a demon in one. Why? Because a church is a pure place where no one dares to cheat or lie or drink or gamble or fornicate." He gestured to the other patrons. "These people do all those things here and that's probably what summoned the demon that attacked you."

The jukebox had stopped playing, and most of the patrons now eyeballed Evans.

"Lakehouse Lounge is actually a devil's playground!" Evans said, raising his voice so all could hear. "Satan sent one of his soldiers here last night, having already paved the way with a myriad of sins and by using weapons such as alcohol and gambling machines and *rock and roll!* I'd say he let Mr. Mc-Cracken and Mr. Widner off relatively lightly. He might not be so merciful next time!"

Evans sensed someone behind him when he stopped to gather his breath and thoughts. He felt the back of his collar being grabbed before he could turn around.

"Time to hit the road, Jack," the bartender growled into his ear.

"Okay, okay. Just don't rip my shirt. And the name's Calvin, not Jack."

"I don't give two shits about your shirt *or* your name."

The bartender began to walk Evans toward the exit.

"*It was Harry McBride, not a demon!*" McCracken yelled after him. "*Don't try to take that from us!*"

The bartender shoved Evans out the door before he could respond to McCracken. Evans remained in the parking lot instead of trying to re-enter the bar, breathless from his impromptu sermon, but also gratified and even exhilarated. Though he hadn't found Harry McBride, nor gotten what he'd consider viable clues to his whereabouts, he felt he'd accomplished something much more significant. The denizens of Lakehouse Lounge had needed to be frightened out of their

sinful ways and he believed he'd done just that. More importantly, he'd helped the Lord do His work. Even He needed a
hand now and then. Evans suspected he'd be rewarded for his
efforts somewhere down the line.

Chapter 11

Harry parked beside a Walmart in Mena, Arkansas as dawn filtered through low, ash-colored clouds. He slouched behind the wheel and slept fitfully while dreaming of a beautiful blind woman feathering her fingertips over his face, her words rendering his features as perfectly and poetically as anyone sighted possibly could. She told Harry his was the handsomest she'd ever touched, and Harry reveled in that until he woke just before noon.

He drove the rest of the day, relieved when evening finally curtained the highway, making him just another pair of headlights. He passed through formless towns bordered by the usual fast food and convenience stores. Wariness of security guards and surveillance cameras deterred him from stopping despite his hunger. Not to mention cops. They seemed be everywhere.

Route 88 merged with Route 71 and ran south through ex-urban sprawl that eventually opened into empty lots which gave way to cornfields farther on. Gently rolling hills replaced the cornfields as late evening blue darkened to black. The road wound between some and cut through others, their jagged granite interiors reinforced by heavy steel mesh.

The land dropped into a densely-wooded valley on the far side of one such hill, its floor marked by a light Harry imagined signaling to him from amidst the trees. He focused on the light and fought the desire to drive through the guardrail toward it. Death urges usually came to him this way, most powerfully when he felt particularly alone and uncertain. This one sent a shudder up his spine and the temperature in the car seemed to plunge despite the warmth blowing through the open window. He pulled over and got out to escape the chill.

Harry moved away from the car and closer to the guardrail, shivering despite the balmy southern air. The beckoning light reminded him of the one over the porch of the lakeside cabin he and Grace had rented in the Catskills. He recalled making love by the fireplace the first night there; the flames casting shadows that danced against the rough-hewn walls, the crackles and pops of the hardwood sounding like laughter. He'd slept deeply and dreamlessly afterward, and had felt unusually peaceful and content in the morning while watching fish nuzzle the lake's glassy surface and the sun breach the mountain on the other side. He'd even wept there beside the still, cool water, sure he'd turned a corner.

"I don't want to die," he said, his words swallowed by the yawning valley before him.

You don't have to. Grace's voice; sure and soothing.

An unseen hand on the back of his neck banished Grace. The hand's grip tightened and Harry felt it pushing him toward the guardrail. He leaned back, then spun around and punched at what turned out to be nothing at all. He threw another punch that found the same void. He kept punching regardless, with both fists, until his arms tired and dropped to his sides.

He returned to the Taurus drenched in sweat and immediately regretted switching on the radio.

"*…Oooh, Haar-ry, come out, come out where-ev-er you aaaare,*" Grover Budd was saying. "*But seriously, folks, I've been accused of obsessing over Harry McBride, of devoting too much time to him and neglecting other important issues. Let me tell you something: Harry McBride IS the issue. THE important issue of the day, of the year, of the decade…*"

Harry turned off the radio and Route 71 took him to Route 265 which brought him to Fayetteville. He parked at a Super 8 Motel on the far side of town, got out, and bent down to stretch his back and hamstrings. Neither loosened much, and his fingertips failed to reach his toes.

A shiny, new-looking BMW pulled in. Harry ducked behind the Taurus and watched a young couple step out of the car; the man clean-cut and self-assured in his button-down and pressed khaki's, the woman's honey-colored hair caressing smooth, tanned shoulders covered only by spaghetti straps. The man draped his arm around those shoulders and the two lovers walked toward the motel entrance giggling at some private joke. Harry watched from the shadows, longing to go with them, to somehow share in the ease and assurance they seemed to possess in such abundance.

He pulled the phone from his pocket.

"*Harry.*"

"Hey, Grace."

"*You shouldn't be calling.*"

"I know. How ya doin'?"

"*'How ya doin?' he asks. How about you?*"

"Could be better."

"*Oh, really? I hear you been living the dream. A woman in every port, like a sailor or something.*"

"Don't believe everything you hear."

"*How many you up to, if you don't mind me askin'?*"

"Just one. She blackmailed me."

"Poor Harry. Which lucky lady was that? Maryland, Massachusetts, or Tennessee?"

"C'mon, Grace, don't bust my balls."

Grace remained silent for several moments.

"Sorry," she said. *"It's none of my business."*

"It is *too* your business, but–"

"No, Harry, it's really not."

Harry bit his lower lip, hoping the pain might cover that caused by Grace's last comment.

"I was just thinking about our honeymoon," he said. "At the cabin by that lake in the Catskills."

"It was nice up there."

"Seems like yesterday."

"We been down Memory Lane before."

Harry eyed a police cruiser on the highway, its headlights beaming accusation.

"I'm gonna get out this mess," he said once the cruiser had passed. "I think I got a good defense if they end up catching me."

Grace laughed humorlessly.

"It's all over the internet and on every channel. What kind of defense could you possibly have?"

"Aggravated something or other. Mental distress. I'll get a lawyer."

Harry heard her place something on a table; a wineglass, he guessed.

"Cops and FBI and reporters are still calling me, ya know. That strange Calvin PI guy, too."

"Like I told you, don't give 'em nothing."

"I tell 'em I got no idea where you are."

"Which is true."

"Let's keep it that way, if you don't mind."

A light in a ground-floor room went on, silhouetting the young couple against a drawn curtain.

"I wish we were together," Harry said, eyeing the silhouettes.

"You had your chances."

"I made you happy, though. Didn't I?"

"Sometimes...for a while."

"I still could."

"I think that train's already left the station."

Harry waited for her to say more.

"I better go before they track my signal," he said when she didn't.

"Good idea."

"But think about it. Think about us being happy and all."

"Okay."

"And the Catskills."

"I will."

"Promise?"

"All right," Grace said, her voice distant and unsure.

"Take care, Grace."

"You, too. Drive carefully, okay?"

Harry ended the call and looked at the window separating him from the couple, their one-dimensional forms embracing now. It reminded him of scene in an old black and white movie, and he smiled while imagining himself in it, playing the role of the man on the other side. *Lucky guy*, he thought, his smile fading with the realization that he'd never been lucky and probably never would be.

Chapter 12

Stanley Siebert rationed the last inch of his coffee even though it had already gone cold and tasted like water. Because he knew he wouldn't be getting a second cup. Not this morning or any other for the foreseeable future. That's because Seibert had to play by his mother-in-law's rules ever since losing his auto plant job six months ago. The kitchen table he sat at belonged to Mother-In-Law, after all. So did the kitchen the table furnished and the house containing the kitchen. Her house. Her kitchen. Her table. Her coffee. *Her fucking rules.* Seibert had given up arguing that brewing a second pot wouldn't exactly break her. He knew damned well it wasn't about money.

Seibert had never paid much attention to the nuances of human behavior, though he did recognize controlling tendencies when he encountered them, especially if *he* happened to be their target. That's why he no longer wondered if dear Mother-In-Law wanted him living there. Of course, she did. Supplying him with Maxwell House for breakfast and mac and cheese for dinner seemed a small price to pay for having a loser son-in-law around to badger and harangue whenever she wanted to.

Seibert planned to finish his coffee and leave before the old lady woke and came downstairs. It seemed like a good idea until he remembered he had nowhere to go and driving there with gasoline pushing $3.00 a gallon would be expensive. He considered calling his wife at work, but he had nothing to say and an average of five calls a day had clearly begun to irritate her almost as much as earning all the money while Mr. Husband moped around her mother's house.

Still, like mother-like daughter, Seibert's wife couldn't completely conceal her satisfaction at having him in such a compromised position. Seibert suspected revenge lay at the root of it. *But for what?* For being a regular guy? For lacking the foresight to develop skills other than those needed by an auto plant? Who the hell could have known they'd ship the whole damned thing to Mexico?

Seibert hoped to finish the paper in peace before the matriarch made her grand entrance and claimed it. He decided to first read the sports section–the most important one–in case she happened to alter her routine and arrive early. The sports pages reported nothing interesting. The Cleveland Indians had failed to make the playoffs and the Browns didn't play until Sunday. He skimmed a recap of a Cavs' pre-season game, then flipped the paper and read the front page article about Harry McBride.

Lucky bastard, he thought after finishing it.

But the more Seibert thought about Harry, the more he realized Harry wasn't lucky at all. Any dope can get lucky. Any idiot can spot a four-leaf clover or pick the right lottery numbers. No, Harry McBride had *made* his luck, taken his own fate into his own hands. If reports about him were true, he was having the time of his life out there on the road. Seibert suspected most American men identified with Harry just as much as he did, each secretly hankering to punch whoever pissed him off before hitting the highway and bedding bored housewives on the way to Mexico; Harry's destination, according to the article and the accompanying map illustrating his likely route.

Seibert closed his eyes and let his imagination take him on his own journey out of this unwelcoming house, away from dying Ashtabula, Ohio, and into the heart of a nation filled with fun and freedom and...*possibility*. His daydream carried him along with Harry McBride, through the Great Plains and across the western deserts where he could see his mother-in-law coming from miles away. They'd turn south from there and over the border they'd go, into a Mexico bathed in sunshine and stocked with warm women who prefer to cook and clean and have sex with their man rather than control and denigrate him.

He studied Harry's work ID photo, which had been transposed onto the map so Route 44 ran right across the man's forehead. Keep going, McBride. Don't let the fuckers catch you. That's exactly what Seibert was thinking when the air in the room shifted ever so slightly. Seibert steeled himself before looking up from the paper at Mother-In-Law, standing before him with hands on hips, a bulky pink terrycloth bathrobe wrapped around her bulky pink body. Matching slippers covered her bunion-ed feet, concealing the gnarled nails sprouting from her misshapen toes. Seibert made sure to return and hold her contempt-shot gaze. Looking away would only give her the victory she so badly craved.

"Check the Help Wanted's yet, Stanley?"

"Not yet."

"So, you're gonna let the men who actually *want* to work get the jobs."

Seibert tapped the newspaper with his index finger

"I can't do any of these."

"You can't or you won't?"

"The real jobs are posted online, not in newspapers," Seibert said. "We don't have wireless in this house."

"I don't need wireless and your internet phone would work if you'd bothered to pay the bill."

Seibert downed the rest of his coffee, as if it might be confiscated at any moment.

"I saw one in here for a home cleaner yesterday. Think I'd be good at scrubbing toilets?"

"You could always start training here."

"There's another for a health care aide. Wipe some geezer's ass for minimum wage."

"I can't think of anything you're more qualified for." A victorious sneer had spread across Mother-In-Law's face.

That sneer froze Seibert's insides and stilled his tongue. Unable to deny Mother-In-Law had gotten the better of the exchange, he averted his eyes while searching for a retort. They settled again on Harry McBride and his panic and despair began to ebb, replaced by strength and resolve that flowed first into Seibert's legs, then into the rest of his body.

Feeling more in control now, Seibert stood and moved from behind the table. He took two deliberate steps toward his robed tormentor, made a fist, and pulled it back. He visualized his fist travelled the remaining distance to Mother-In-Law's face and Mother-In-Law collapsing like a lightning-struck tree. But Mother-In-Law swung before Seibert did, her open palm landing hard and flush against his left ear. Stunned more than hurt, Seibert lowered his fist to his side and retreated behind the table, his legs feeling weak and unsteady. So, he sat again and looked down into his empty coffee cup, his chin resting on his deflated chest, his boxed ear ringing, his briefly resurgent spirit crushed by Mother-In-Law's blow.

Chapter 13

Josh Weinberg earned an easy $300 by telling Calvin Evans exactly where Harry had last called Grace McBride from. Not a difficult task, since Verizon happened to pay the Fayetteville, Arkansas Super 8 a hefty annual fee for the relay it had installed on its roof.

Evans followed Weinberg's information to a soul food joint called Momma Dean's, located three miles north of the Fayetteville Super 8. He drove all day to get there and hoped the Bible might help settle the nerves tickling the pit of his belly as he parked and prepared to go inside. Evans never had issues with one or two African-Americans at a time; being surrounded by them–as he assumed he would be in Momma Dean's–had always made him uneasy. He opened the Bible to Psalm 23:4, one of his favorites.

Senator Landon called before he could read it.

"Hiya, Joe."

"Where are you?"

"Fayetteville."

"North Carolina?"

"Arkansas."

"Didn't know there was an Arkansas Fayetteville. What's your status?"

"I'm starting to get a sense for McBride, a real *taste* for him."

"I'd imagine the key to finding him is going to where he is, not tasting him. Keep me posted."

"Will do, sir."

Evans pushed the "End" button and returned to Psalm 23:4.

"Yea, though I walk through the valley of the shadow of death, I will fear no evil; for You are with me; Your rod and Your staff, they comfort me."

He felt like reciting the passage again, this time altering the ending to "I will fear no evil; for I am the baddest motherfucker in the valley," as he and some of his ex-colleagues at FBI would before dangerous operations. Evans held his tongue, unwilling to disrespect the Book anymore. He got out of the minivan, entered Momma Dean's, and headed straight to the bar.

"My man," he said to the bartender after settling onto a stool.

The bartender looked at Evans as if he'd never served a white customer, especially one trying to sound ghetto. He shifted a toothpick from one side of his mouth to the other.

"Can I getcha?"

Evans hesitated, club soda and lime ready but unable to roll off the tip of his tongue. AA testimonies had taught him this is how it happens, how even the most resolute members fall off the wagon. Neither a big event nor a dramatic moment usually precipitates the lapse, but rather one of weakness or fear or perceived vulnerability. Evans felt a combination of all three now that the demographics in Momma Dean's had, indeed, made him a minority of one.

"Courvoisier and Coke," he told the bartender before he could stop himself. "I'm sure you make lots of them."

The bartender rolled his eyes at Evans' race-based assumption before going to fix the drink. Evans took a mouthful when it arrived, the unfamiliar yet familiar heat hitting his unaccustomed body as soon as he swallowed. He decided to enjoy instead of fight the sensation, and even considered for the first time since going sober that moderation might be more realistic than abstinence in the long run. Better to bend like a reed in a storm than be blown over like an oak, he thought, unsure if he'd read that in the Bible or not. Either way, *I'm gonna bend like a motherfuckin' reed tonight.*

He turned around on his stool and studied Momma Dean's customers, sure most had police records. He considered issuing one of his patented cop glares to keep them at bay. The firm-looking posterior belonging to one of the waitresses soon captured his attention, pulling his eyes across the dining room along with it.

Damn!

He drank more Courvoisier and Coke, which wafted from his stomach into his sinuses, where it briefly lingered before continuing to his brain. He tuned into the Seventies soul playing on the jukebox in the side room; it reminded him of the African-American woman who used to clean his house when he was a child, how she'd hum to similar music on her transistor radio as she mopped and dusted and made beds.

The woman's son, Kevin, often accompanied his mother on her weekly visits, and Kevin and Evans would play for hours while she worked. Evans recalled how they'd hit baseballs in summer and throw the football in fall and shoot baskets all year round. But their play dates became less frequent as the years passed and Kevin grew old enough to recognize the racial divide between them. The boy eventually stopped visiting altogether, making young Evans feel slighted and abandoned and confused. Nowadays, in rare moments of introspection and even rarer moments of clarity, he realized that's when his attitude toward African-Americans took a turn he couldn't seem to correct, no matter how hard he tried to.

He finished his drink and waved the bartender over again.

"What's your name, bro?"

"Darrell."

"Cool name. I like it. A-ight, Darrell. I'll get down to bidness. I'm a private investigator looking for a man named McBride, the one who hit Senator Landon upside the head."

"*Harry* McBride?"

"The one and only."

"Why you lookin' for him here?"

"Because he made a call at the Super 8 down the road recently. I think he might have come to Momma Dean's either before or after."

Darrell's jaw muscles bulged and contracted as he pulped his toothpick between his molars.

"Makes you think that?"

"He supposedly likes to eat your kind food, for one. And, as I just said, he used his cell phone at the Super 8." Evans touched his temple. "Put two and two together."

Darrell briefly pondered this information.

"If he called at the Super 8, why ain't you harassing folks over there?"

Evans searched for an answer that wouldn't divulge the main reason he'd come to Momma Dean's first. Because no matter how often and hard he tried to convince himself that he liked and respected African-Americans, he actually couldn't help fearing and loathing yet feeling hopelessly drawn to them.

"Don't worry, I'll be harassing at the Super 8 soon enough," he said. "I'll need a straight answer from you first. A guy like McBride would stand out like a sore thumb here, am I right?"

"Just like you."

"You didn't answer my question."

"Why would I tell you even if I *had* seen him?"

"Call me naïve, but I like to think at least some of you people are on the side of law and order."

Darrell looked ready to spit across the bar.

"How do I know you're really a PI?"

"I prefer not to flash my badge in a place like this, to be honest."

"Your badge wouldn't mean shit, anyway. You ain't a cop."

"Okay, I get it. Plea the fifth. It's your constitutional right. I'll just drink another Courvoisier and Coke and let you think it over."

Evans turned his back to Darrell and laser-ed onto the waitress's butt again. He tracked it into the side room, where some patrons were dancing by the jukebox. The bastards *do* have rhythm, Evans thought. He started bobbing his head to the music, way off beat. He kept at it regardless, struggling to find flow. Though the alcohol had loosened his mind, his body remained tight and any flow he did possess stayed locked away. He tried snapping his fingers, but they refused to synchronize with the song, and the discordant sound they made drew curious looks.

The waitress he'd been scoping took a seat at the end of the bar a half hour later, her butt and blackness mitigating Evans' usual lack of interest in women beyond their teens. Darrell brought the woman a vodka and orange. Evans's watched her lips envelop the tiny stirrer straw.

Shi-it!

He drank more Courvoisier and Coke, and it soon gave him enough nerve to saunter down the bar and angle into the space beside the waitress. She failed to notice him until he said, "You're lookin' real fine tonight."

The waitress kept her eyes on the top shelf bottles and blew some fatigue from the side of her mouth.

"I mean one *foxy lady*," Evans persisted.

The waitress's eyes dropped from the bottles to her drink.

"I'm only having one," she said. "Then I'm going home."

"C'mon, baby, I'm a customer. That means you have to be nice to me."

"I'm off-duty."

"What a coincidence? So am I."

The waitress glanced over at Darrell, then looked at Evans.

"What would it take for you to not be standing here talking to me?"

That took some but not all the wind out of Evans' sails.

"How about you and me go over to the jukebox and cut a rug?" he said. "I'm feeling the music in me tonight."

"You sure it's not the booze you're feeling?"

Evans held up his glass.

"Courvoisier and Coke. Drink of kings."

Darrell came over.

"Everything awright?"

"We're cool," Evans answered for both of them.

Darrell hovered in the vicinity a moment or two before heading back down the bar.

"One dance, then I'll leave," Evans said to the waitress.

The woman laughed to cover her exasperation.

"You don't quit, do you?"

Evans slid into his minivan twenty minutes later, and sat gripping the wheel with both hands instead of starting it. The waitress had finally agreed to dance, prompting him to believe his night had turned lucky. That is until he realized he danced even worse on his feet than on a stool. Not that he'd forgotten how; he'd never learned, neither at the Sweet Sixteens or proms he'd attended as a kid, nor at the more recent weddings. He'd always plant himself on the sidelines at those awkward affairs, nervously cracking jokes and talking sports with the other rhythmically challenged wallflowers.

He punched the wheel, but the pain that caused failed to dispel visions of himself struggling before Momma Dean's jukebox with his front teeth clamped over his lower lip, his arms pumping mechanically while his feet shot every which way. He hadn't actually heard the music; he'd been too busy concentrating on his moves and performing all the worse for it. He'd collided with another dancer during one song, accidently jabbing his elbow into the man's sternum. He'd lost balance while spinning during another song, crashing into the jukebox and making it skip. He'd noticed the waitress smiling at him at one point. This had lifted his hopes, but only until he'd realized the smile was actually a suppressed laugh. The waitress had managed to evade Evans each time he'd lurched toward her, and Darrell had shown up just after Evans had decided he'd done enough dancing to have earned a kiss.

Evans refused to cry, although crying is exactly what he felt like doing. *Don't give them one fucking tear, Calvin.* He could still hear the laughter and hoots that had trailed him out of Momma Dean's into the parking lot, where Darrell had escorted him even more roughly than the Lakehouse Lounge bartender had. Evans again tried to convince himself that stopping at the soul food restaurant had been all about tracking Harry McBride. Reports *did* indicate the man enjoyed barbeque, which is similar to soul food. And McBride *had* been in the vicinity, at least according to Josh Weinberg.

He opened the Bible to Leviticus 25:44:

However, you may purchase male or female slaves from among the foreigners who live among you. You may also purchase the children of such resident foreigners, including those who have been born in your land. You may treat them as your property, passing them on to your children as a permanent inheritance...

He looked through the windshield at Momma Dean's and again heard its customers laughing at him.

"You may treat them as your property," he quoted before turning to Ephesian 6:5:

Slaves, obey your earthly masters with deep respect and fear. Serve them sincerely as you would serve Christ.

He imagined the crowded restaurant burning to the ground. On to Luke 12:47:

The servant will be severely punished, for though he knew his duty, he refused to do it.

Evans flipped to the Book of Job next, but decided to read it only when he'd reached a true precipice. He felt close to one now, but not quite at the edge. He shut the Book and returned it to the passenger seat. The smoothing effect of Courvoisier had started to dissipate, leaving a jangled-ness in its wake. The Bible passages had made Evans feel a little better regardless; more centered and grounded. They'd also helped cordon much of his anger and humiliation and direct them back toward their source. The Bible had always managed to rescue him from these depths, to correct his wayward paths. He looked down at the Book and tears of gratitude filled his eyes. For he knew It would always be there to guide him through his situations–good, bad, and ugly. He knew It would always be there through all his trials and all his tribulations.

Chapter 14

Route 7 straightens and flattens and runs roughly parallel to the equator soon after it clears Duncan, Oklahoma. Harry followed the vacant highway west as evening fell over the scrublands. He drove in a fatigue trance toward the burnt orange horizon, his index finger steadying the wheel of the Maxima he'd swapped for the Taurus back in Wilburton.

He'd already turned on the radio and Grover Budd's voice now slithered from the speakers, battling the ruffling of warm wind past the open window.

"…An unemployed auto worker in Ashtabula, Ohio called in earlier to complain about losing his job. Turns out he really wanted to complain about his mother-in-law bitch-slapping him for no apparent reason. Now you tell me what Harry McBride did to Senator Landon had no influence on that."

"Guys get bitch-slapped every day in this country," Adam, a caller from Joplin, Missouri, replied, his accent a mixture of midwestern flat and southern twang.

"But by mother-in-laws?" Budd said.

"Sure, why not?"

"*Okay, Adam, on average, how many American men get bitch-slapped by their mother-in-law on a daily basis? Give me stats.*"

"*I can't give stats, Grover, but I'm pretty sure Harry had absolutely nothing to do with it.*"

"Damned straight, I didn't," Harry said.

"*Ever heard of zeitgeist?*" Budd said. "*Because that man was undoubtedly a victim of the violent, anarchistic zeitgeist inspired by Harry McBride and currently spreading like wildfire across the nation. Which is exactly what McBride's Democrat Party sponsors want. Create a chaotic void, then step in and fill it with jack-booted control.*"

Budd ended the call and took another.

"*Speak, American listener. Tell Grover what's going horribly wrong with our God forsaken country.*"

"*Grover, this is Maude from Tempe, Arizona.*"

"*Oh my gawd, it's Maude! What's bothering you, Maude?*"

"*I hear Harry McBride's been stopping at barbeque restaurants.*"

"*I've heard that, too, from several of my sources.*"

"*He may have also eaten at a soul food place in Fayetteville, Arkansas.*"

I wish I had, Harry thought, starting to feel hungry.

"*Okay, Maude, I see where you're going. What we have is a socialist-o-path named Harry McBride who hit the Republican presidential candidate, then fled. Does he eat at white places like Stuckey's or Bob's Big Boy or Cracker Barrel while on the lam? Noooooo! Mr. McBride makes a point of eating black food in black restaurants, his way of signaling solidarity with the people he's clearly chosen to champion, a race war dog whistle if I ever heard one.*"

"Gimme a break," Harry said.

"*Harry eating soul food while running from the law is a clear, unequivocal incitation to social unrest, even rioting,*" Budd added.

"Did you know the origins of barbeque and soul food can be traced directly to the slaves?" Maude said. *"I happened to Google it this morning."*

"Good work, Maude. Let's look at the bigger picture. We've had a black Democrat in the Oval Office for nearly eight years. Given that, do you think it's a coincidence Harry McBride assaulted a Republican senator from one of the whitest states in the nation, then goes eating stacks of ribs and mounds of collard greens and buckets of black-eyed peas and whatever the hell else those black establishments serve?"

"No coincidence at all, Grover."

"Thanks for calling and raising such interesting and important points, Maude."

Budd's description of soul food had stoked Harry's appetite even more. He'd often sample the leftover collard greens and corn bread and black-eyed peas Nate Branch, his closest friend at Sargeant, would bring for lunch. He wondered what Nate thought of him now.

Jeff from Wichita Falls, Texas got through next.

"Jeff from Wichita Falls, Texas. I reckon you called because you have a bee in your Texas bluebonnet today."

"Hi, Grover. I actually wanted to address something hardly anyone else ever does."

"Addressing what no one else does is why the Grover Budd Show–the most widely listened-to radio show in the land–exists. What's bothering you, Jeff?"

"What's bothering me is the fact that ninety-five percent of the blacks in this country voted for the current president in the last two elections."

"It is a fact and an absolutely true one at that," Budd said. *"But what's significant about it? What does it mean?"*

"It means those people are flat-out racist."

"Hang on. Wait just a minute. I thought so-called 'African-Americans' were incapable of being racist."

"They sure as heck can be. And they have the nerve to call US racist."

"The pot calling the kettle black, as it were."

"And the Liberal Media insists the blacks voted for the current president because he's a Democrat like they are, not because he's the same race. Do you believe that?"

"Not for a cotton pickin' second."

A billboard advertising Big Steak Restaurant, in nearby Amarillo, caught Harry's attention, particularly its offer of a free 72oz London broil plus $500 for anyone able to eat it. A second Big Steak billboard appeared several miles later, the London broil image on it causing Harry's stomach to pang. He listened to Budd more closely in order to distract himself from his hunger, and couldn't believe his ears when the radio host promised his listeners irrefutable evidence that Harry McBride had secretly met with the president only days before attacking Landon.

Another billboard loomed against the fading sunset five miles on. Harry expected it to offer more beef enticement, but a man's face rather than a steak graphic dominated this advertisement. The closing distance gradually transformed the face from generic into one he recognized all too well. That's because the exact same face adorned the Sargeant employee ID card in his front pocket.

"What the fuck!"

Harry grabbed the wheel with both hands to keep from driving off the road. He looked at himself in the rearview and quickly compared his real features to the giant pixelated ones plastered across the top of the billboard.

"The Harry McBride Society: Fighting for a fair, decent, and honest America. Save your country by donating just $1 at www.harrymcbridesociety.com" occupied the space beneath his image, and "Visit HMS on Facebook, Instagram, and Twitter" anchored the bottom of the sign.

"Holy... Fucking... Christ!"

Sweat prickled Harry's brow and adrenaline weighted his foot, causing the Maxima to zoom past the billboard at 92 miles an hour. Harry felt helpless to slow down, as if he no longer controlled the car and had become a mere passenger in it. He considered going back for another look, to make sure his eyes and mind hadn't been playing tricks. No need to, as it turned out. A second Harry McBride Society billboard soon appeared, this one only a quarter mile beyond another for Big Steak Restaurant.

Chapter 15

New York City, NY (Day 16)

Grover Budd nursed a Ketel One martini at a secluded table in Peacock Alley, the dimly-lit restaurant off the Waldorf Astoria lobby. He'd finished half the cocktail by the time a hostess brought Chris Watkins over.

"He'll have one of these," Budd told the woman, tapping the rim of his glass.

"How'd you know?" Watkins said.

"You seem like a martini guy."

"I'll take that as a compliment." Watkins sat. "You look well."

"Let's wait for your drink."

They remained awkwardly silent until a raven-haired waitress in a short black skirt delivered it. Budd eyed her back to the bar.

"She's got a pair of legs, that one," he said.

"Most people do."

"Not like those."

Watkins sampled his martini.

"Anyway, nice to see you, Grover."

"You're one of the few who still use the word 'nice' and 'Grover' in the same sentence."

"You're a pearl before swine. Don't forget that."

"Flattery works, amigo. Keep it up."

Watkins sipped more martini.

"Good drink."

"It's the reason I come here. One reason, anyway."

"Here's the thing: We want you to sell fear."

"I already do."

"But we want you to harness and steer it toward us."

Budd imagined fear as one of those giant, undulating soap bubbles, its shape and direction subject to even the faintest wind.

"Landon know about this?"

"It was his idea."

"Then what's he paying you for?"

Watkins smiled through the insult, the muted chandelier light playing off his unnaturally straight, unnaturally white teeth.

"Schwartz is going to confiscate guns if he wins the election," he said.

"That's pretty basic, Chris."

"But it goes to the heart of the matter. Landon, on the other hand, has an A rating from the NRA."

Budd glanced at the bar, then looked at Watkins again.

"The problem is Schwartz isn't really planning to confiscate guns. He's from a rural state."

"He does want to make it harder for insane people and those on the terrorist watch list to get them. Nothing wrong with that, but it's a slippery slope."

"I wish him luck *slipping* that through Congress," Budd said.

Watkins smiled with a bit less wattage this time.

"Health insurance."

"What about it?"

"Schwartz wants the federal government to take it over and force people to buy it. Landon believes in freedom of choice. Government control on one hand, individual liberty on the other."

Budd blew out his cheeks, making no effort to conceal his boredom.

"Noted. What else?"

"Harry McBride. You've been devoting a lot of air time to him."

"Can't make this shit up."

"Any way you can you tie him to the Schwartz campaign more concretely than just speculation and innuendo?"

"I could tie him to the Kennedy assassinations if I wanted to."

"Which reminds me. Violent crime. Simply put, Schwartz will be soft on it and Landon will be tough."

Budd sipped his martini, which had warmed to nearly room temperature.

"Hate to break it to you, but crime's been dropping for decades."

"Perception is it's rising. Did you know that?"

"I might not be from the east coast like you, Chris, but I didn't just fall off a turnip truck."

"Regarding crime, we're not asking you to turn your show into a daily blotter. Just mention one or two each day, particularly those committed by illegal aliens or homegrown minorities."

"Homegrown minority's going to be us white guys pretty soon. At least *my* kind of white guy."

Watkins let the dig at his sexuality pass.

"That's another talking point," he said. "The beleaguered white guy facing a growing and hostile army of everyone who isn't a beleaguered white guy. Don't overlook the economy, either."

"It's been improving for years, unfortunately."

"Doesn't matter. Use anecdotes of inner city blight. Paint verbal pictures of societal collapse that only a strong, experienced, level-headed president like Joe Landon can prevent."

"People hoarding food and water."

"While vicious criminals roam the land."

"Killing you, then having the courtesy to rape your wife afterward," Budd said with a grin.

Watkins placed his hand on his stomach.

"Play to their guts, not their brains."

"That's what's made me a millionaire, my friend."

Call girls had started to populate the bar, reminding Budd of birds gathering on a telephone wire at dusk.

"Terrorism," Watkins said, after patting his lips with the cocktail napkin and smoothing it on the table.

"Terrorism's my favorite hobby."

"Remind people that a liberal like Schwartz won't protect them from bad guys in turbans, especially since he's probably on *their* side."

Listening to advice about his own show had started to rankle Budd. The flaring hips of a call girl in a green dress caught his eye.

"I get it," he said.

Watkins checked to make sure no one was within earshot.

"Let's talk money then."

This re-captured most of Budd's attention.

"Cash, obviously."

"I'd think checks and wires from the Landon campaign might raise a red flag or two."

"It would only confirm what everyone already suspects." Budd's eyes resumed skiing the call girl's hips. "Let me ask you something, Chris. How does a man of your type bring himself to work for someone like Landon?"

Watkins sat up straighter.

"What do you mean 'my type'?"

"I mean, of your sexual *persuasion*, for lack of a better word."

Watkins drank more martini.

"I suppose I could ask a similar question about what you do."

Budd looked over at the green dress again.

"I'm not saying there's anything wrong with it. I'm just saying most people like you would be working for the other side."

"I'm on my own side, Grover. That's the only one that matters to me."

Budd pulled his eyes from the call girl and fixed them on Watkins.

"That makes two of us."

Budd paid the check and left only a $5 tip for the waitress, incentive for her to do something more productive with her life. He accompanied Watkins to the lobby, where they shook hands and agreed to reconvene at the end of the month. He waited until Watkins had turned the corner past the rare book store before doubling back to Peacock Ally and claiming the empty stool beside the woman he'd been admiring. She sat with a highball that Budd guessed contained seltzer and lime.

"Ketel One, Mr. Cotton?" the bartender asked.

"You read my mind, Steven."

Budd climbed onto the stool and inhaled the woman's perfume while watching Steven shake the shaker over one shoulder then over the other before straining its contents into a thin-stemmed glass.

"You have the hands of a surgeon, Steven," Budd said as the vodka settled and clarified.

"Practice, Mr. Cotton."

The radio host sipped the icy booze down from the rim.

"Aahh!" he exhaled, loudly enough for his neighbor to hear.

"Sounds like you enjoy martinis," she said, taking Budd's bait while setting her own.

"I actually enjoy chilled vodka with a touch of dry vermouth. A true martini is *gin* and dry vermouth."

"Learn something new every day."

Budd turned to the woman, whose beauty made his breath catch.

"Anyone ever tell you you're the spitting image of Linda Carter?" he said after his lungs had regained function. "She played Wonder Woman in the Seventies."

"That was a little before my time."

"A little after mine, I'm afraid."

The woman's emerald eyes met and held Budd's.

"I think most men are more attractive *after* their time."

Budd offered his hand.

"Bill Cotton."

"Janice."

"You should have told me we weren't doing last names, Janice."

"Seems like I have the advantage now."

"I don't know about that, but I do know you've almost finished your soda. Can I buy you a real drink?"

They ate dinner in Peacock Alley after finishing their cocktails, making small talk over appetizers and remaining mostly silent during the main courses. Budd considered the meal practice for his rare dates with non-professionals. They went upstairs after the meal, the room he'd already reserved decorated with taupe upholstered furniture that matched the bedding and complimented the crimson wallpaper, which imparted a touch of bordello. Budd hung his blazer in the closet and sat on the sofa facing the bed. Janice remained standing, awaiting instructions.

"Why don't you unwrap your wrap dress?" Budd said.

"I'm impressed. Most men wouldn't know what type of dress this is."

"I'm what you call a dedicated follower of fashion."

Janice undid her dress and hung it beside Budd's blazer.

"Your bra and panties, too," Budd said. "Then get on the bed."

The call girl did, and Budd's breath shallowed as he admired the lush, flawless nudity stretched before him. He joined Janice on the bed, positioned his lips over her left nipple, and suctioned it past his teeth. He circled his tongue around it for the next several minutes, first clockwise, then counter-clockwise, the robotic activity allowing his mind to go blissfully blank.

"Lots of people love me," he said after releasing the nipple.

"That's nice."

"The problem is far more people despise me. You don't know who I am, do you?"

"You said your name's Bill Cotton."

"And you said your name's Janice. Ever heard of Grover Budd?"

"Of course."

"Do you listen to him?"

"Not often."

"Well, you are now. And if you tell anyone about this, your pimp or whoever, I'm fully capable of making your life living hell. Other nipple, please."

Janice rolled onto her other side so Grover could take her right nipple into his mouth. He sucked it harder than he had the left, and he circled his tongue around it faster. He finally stopped and unzipped his pants.

"All I want you to do is watch, listen, and repeat after me." He reached through the open fly and grasped his member. "Easiest, cleanest trick you've ever turned."

"If that's what you want."

"It's *exactly* what I want. Here we go. I'm a kind man. Say it."

"You're a kind man."

"Good girl. I expected you to say '*I'm* a kind man,' like a parrot. Seems you're a little smarter than a parrot. Okay, I'm a kind, decent, generous man."

"You're a kind, decent, generous man."

Budd began to stroke himself into semi-hardness.

"Who's devoted to his country."

"Who's devoted to his country."

"And to helping his fellow Americans."

"And to helping his fellow Americans."

Budd sat up and made a "T" with his fingertips against his palm.

"Time out. Have you ever done anything like this?"

"No."

"You must think I'm a freak."

"No, I don't."

Budd reclined and grasped himself again.

"Where were we? Kind, generous, devoted helper of fellow Americans. Great man. I'm a great man."

"You're a great man."

Budd's own words issued by the woman's silky-sounding voice put some starch back into his flagging member.

"I'm a true leader."

"You're a true leader."

"Who leads with sound ideas *and* ideals."

"Who leads with sound ideas *and* ideals."

"While refusing to succumb to the prevailing winds of idiocy."

"While refusing to succumb to the…what was that?"

"Prevailing winds of idiocy."

"Prevailing winds of idiocy."

Budd had achieved a full hard-on by now. He strengthened his grip and pumped it faster.

"I'm a courageous man."

"You're a courageous man."

"Who's going to conquer the world."

"Who's going to conquer the world."

"People respect me."

"People respect you."

"People love me."

"People love you."

"*You* love me."

Janice hesitated.

"*I* love you."

"Like you mean it, please."

"I *love* you."

Those three words did it, releasing a burst of semen into Budd's palm. It quickly seeped through his fingers onto his jutting belly, then rolled off onto the bedspread. His penis and the rest of his body instantly went limp and he lay still except for his rapidly rising and falling chest, the thick thatch of hair matting it drenched in sweat. He kept his eyes on Janice's naked body, making sure not to look at her face. He could use her again another night if he managed to forget her face.

"How much I owe you?"

"A hundred for dinner and two hundred for whatever this was."

"Seems a little high. Okay, clean me up."

Janice stood and went into the bathroom. Budd remained on the bed listening to her washing her hands in the sink, then pulling tissues from the dispenser. He took three hundreds from his wallet and looked up at the ceiling, his sperm cooling on his stomach and Janice's "I *love* you" burning in his head that had started to ache. He began to weep as he waited for the call girl to return. He hadn't wept in years and didn't know why he wept now, not until he realized it was because it no longer bothered him that no woman had ever told him "I love you" for free.

Chapter 16

Amarillo, TX (Day 16)

72 ounces of raw beef greeted Harry when he entered Big Steak Restaurant. The huge London broil rested like a king on a throne of crushed ice, signed photos of those who'd managed to eat similar ones decorating the wall behind it.

"Welcome to Big Steak!" said a beaming blonde hostess in a white cowgirl hat. "Here for the challenge?"

Harry turned to her and instinctively tugged his cap lower. "Yeah, well…maybe."

"You know the rules?"

"I think so."

"I'll repeat 'em for ya, anyway. To win the five hundred dollars *and* get your fifty-dollar deposit back, you have to eat a five-pound steak in an hour or less. You also have to eat a garden salad, a jumbo shrimp cocktail, and a baked potato. Wash it down with a big ol' Coke!"

Harry knew he should leave.

"The signs on the highway didn't say nothing about salad and shrimp and baked potato and Coke," he said. "They didn't say nothing about a fifty-dollar deposit and doing it in an hour, neither."

"You can drink Sprite or Mountain Dew instead, if you like," the hostess offered.

Harry glanced at the hubcap-sized steak.

"You would pay me in cash, right?"

"Sure thing. But if you want to go ahead with the challenge, you'll have to sign a waiver first."

"A waiver?"

"Alls it says is we're not responsible if you throw up or pass out or have to go to the hospital." The hostess slid one across the podium. "It also says your family can't sue us if you die."

Harry gauged the steak again; his favorite meal. He scribbled "Joe Williams" on the waiver despite his misgivings and handed the waitress two twenties and a ten; most of his remaining funds.

"All right, we're good to go!"

The hostess locked Harry's money and waiver in the podium drawer before leading him into a cavernous dining room jammed with tables hemmed by patrons and laden with steaks and burgers, pitchers of beer and soda, baskets of fries and onion rings. Harry followed her through the noisy throng up onto a small, round stage at the center of the room.

The hostess donned a wireless microphone headset.

"Listen up, ladies and gents! Tonight Joe Williams here's gonna take the Big Steak Challenge! *Woo-hoo!*"

WOO-HOO! the crowd echoed.

"And maybe earn himself membership in the Big Steak Club!"

WOO-HOO!

"For y'all who don't know how it works, if Joe eats the five-pound steak, the baked potato, the shrimp cocktail, the garden salad, *and* drinks the supersize Coke, he gets it all for free, plus his fifty-dollar deposit back. If he eats everything in *an hour or less*, he also gets *FIVE…HUNDRED…DOLLARS!*"

WOO-HOO!

The hostess directed Harry to sit at the lone table on the stage.

"We'll have your dinner in a jiffy, Mr. Williams." She faced the crowd again. "*Eat that steak, Joe!*"

The crowd immediately started to chant:

EAT THAT STEAK, JOE!
EAT THAT STEAK!
EAT THAT STEAK, JOE!
EAT THAT STEAK!

A burly server in a cowboy shirt and ten-gallon hat arrived ten minutes later. He hauled an enormous platter of food up onto the stage.

"Can I have beer instead of Coke?" Harry asked.

The server lowered a giant pre-cooked steak in front of him.

"Beer's against the rules, Mr. Williams."

"I don't really like shrimp, to be honest."

The server patted Harry's shoulder.

"You'll do fine, buddy."

The man finished offloading the tray, then activated a digital timer and left Harry alone above the crowd that had resumed its chant:

EAT THAT STEAK, JOE!
EAT THAT STEAK!

EAT THAT STEAK, JOE!
EAT THAT STEAK!

Harry had already lost much of his appetite, and the ache in his right hand returned when he gripped the serrated knife the server had provided. He sawed into the steak, relieved to at least find it cooked medium-well, the way he preferred. He shoved a large chunk into his mouth, making sure not to waste time chewing too much before swallowing.

EAT THAT STEAK, JOE!
EAT THAT STEAK!
EAT THAT STEAK, JOE!
EAT THAT STEAK!

Harry planned to finish the meat first, his jaw and stomach working in tandem to process and stow it. He removed his cap and forearmed away sweat that had formed on his brow. His internal temperature kept rising, so he took off his shirt next and continued eating in just his white sleeveless. He realized his error as soon as he noticed a man seated near the stage squinting up at him.

Mind your own business, asshole!

The man kept looking at Harry, who experienced a helpless, sinking feeling when the man turned and whispered into his wife's ear. The wife pushed a forkful of macaroni salad past her lips, and her heavily-mascaraed eyes drifted up to Harry as she chewed. She began to nod once they settled on the tattoo illustrating Harry's exposed right forearm.

The husband shot to his feet, armed with his wife's unspoken affirmation.

"It's Harry McBride!" he cried, pointing at Harry.

No one heard him above the din, except for the family at the next table. Mom, dad, big brother, and little sis all paused their gorge and gawked mutely at the infamous steak-eater. Harry suspected they wouldn't remain mute for long, but knew escaping the restaurant would be difficult now that he'd been recognized. That combined with losing his fifty dollar deposit and not winning the five hundred kept him in his seat eating.

The chant gradually altered as Harry's true identity spread through the room:

EAT THAT STEAK, HARRY!

EAT THAT STEAK!

EAT THAT STEAK, HARRY!

EAT THAT STEAK!

Harry finished the thing in thirty-five minutes and twenty-eight seconds. He started on the potato next and gulped Coke to get it down.

The crowd had shortened and quickened its chant:

EAT, HARRY, EAT!

EAT, HARRY, EAT!

Harry wiped his face with a flimsy paper napkin and struggled to breathe as his expanding belly pressed his ribcage.

The chant grew louder:

EAT, HARRY, EAT!

EAT, HARRY, EAT!

Harry wondered what Grace would say if she could see him now; he decided he'd rather not know. He finished the potato and started on the shrimp, the briny flavor and sulfuric odor nearly making him gag. Only nine minutes and fourteen seconds remained by the time he'd managed to swallow the last one.

Fists had started to pound tables:

EAT, HARRY, EAT!
EAT, HARRY, EAT!

The pounding and chanting inspired Harry to lift the bowl of iceberg lettuce coated in bright orange dressing and shovel it into his mouth with his left hand. He vanquishing the salad in three scoops, then sucked in the final two inches of Coke, clamped his eyes and jaw shut, and willed himself not to vomit.

The timer rang less than a minute later:

HAR-RY! HAR-RY! HAR-RY!
HAR-RY! HAR-RY! HAR-RY!

Harry opened his eyes to the sight of nearly every Big Steak patron standing and either clapping or pumping a fist. Several had squared off to trade air punches. The hostess reappeared and bounded up the steps.

"Harry McBride, ladies and gentlemen!" She grasped and raised Harry's arm. "Newest winner of the *Big Steak Challenge!*"

The restaurant exploded into whoops and hollers. Harry managed to smile and wave as the hostess escorted him from the stage through his now cheering fans. She guided Harry to the bar area, where a smiling manager in a lime-colored Oxford gave him five hundred dollars before directing the hostess and a waitress to snuggle up to him for the requisite photo.

Harry remained in the bar afterward, warily signing autographs and shaking hands with departing diners. He sat on a stool and rested his head on the bar once the last had left, his gurgling belly struggling to retain its cargo. A poem still managed to weave through his fast-fading consciousness:

They think I'm a hero, Grace, but you know I'm really a zero. They think I'm a hero, but I'm just a man running scared…

Harry woke a half hour later when the hostess touched the small of his back. The restaurant had emptied except for bus-boys clearing tables and porters mopping and dishwashers working through piles of dirty plates and cutlery.

The hostess no longer wore her cowgirl hat or her cowgirl smile.

"You okay, Harry?"

Harry's legs felt rubbery when he stood, forcing him to lean against the bar.

"I'm good, I think."

"You sure?"

"I'm my own worst enemy."

The hostess looked across the dining room that appeared smaller empty.

"I'm supposed to act like eating that steak's all fun and games. Someone's gonna have a heart attack one of these days. Or bust a gut."

Harry touched his own gut. It felt as hard and nearly as big as a basketball.

"I'm surprised none of them's dropped a dime on me yet."

"I did read there's a reward for anyone who turns you in. Everyone seemed on your side, though."

Harry looked at the hostess and detected sadness that had been hidden beneath her professional cheer.

"Money has a way of changing minds," he said.

"I wouldn't hang around here much longer then." The hostess placed her hand on Harry's forearm, covering his tattoo with it. "My name's Mary. You have somewhere to stay tonight?"

Chapter 17

The pain emanating from Joe Landon's fractured tailbone made him wince with each step he took. He shuffled one more lap from the window to the bookcase before returning to his desk and calling Chris Watkins.

"Close the door," he said when his campaign manager arrived.

"Aren't we supposed to have an *open* door policy?"

"Only for certain lobbyists and donors."

"Let's hope the Schwartz campaign hasn't bugged your fichus plant, because that would make a heckuva soundbite." Watkins closed the door and sat. "What's on your mind?"

"Harry McBride."

"Elusive."

"I'll say."

"Now there's this Harry McBride Society thing."

"The Wall Street Journal reports Rex Tarsh is one of its backers," Landon said, shaking his head.

"I thought Rex promised to back *us*."

"Maybe he is, in an indirect way." Landon cast a suspicious eye at his fichus, as if the Schwartz campaign *had* bugged it. "All right, here goes: I want to replace Tibbens with McBride."

Watkins didn't react at first.

"Wait. *What?*"

"I want to swap Earl Tibbens for Harry McBride as my VP. Earl can withdraw for some vague personal reason."

Watkins waited for a punchline.

"You're serious," he said when none came.

"As a heart attack."

"McBride's a fugitive, in case you forgot."

"Ever heard of a pardon?"

"He hasn't even been caught, much less convicted."

"Dropping charges is what I mean."

Watkins crossed his legs and began to bounce his right foot against the carpet.

"Then what? Before you answer, first help me understand why this idea, if you consider it that, is a good one."

Landon bent forward over his desk, causing his tailbone to bark.

"Because McBride's a man who people seem to love the shit out of."

"Loving the shit out of someone's way different than—"

"From everything I'm hearing, including from you, people not only love him, they want to *be* him, which means they'd probably vote for him, which would obviously be a vote for me."

The motor jiggling Watkins's foot went into higher gear.

"I realize I might have gotten you all jazzed with those poll numbers."

"Inspired's a better word."

Watkins took a deep breath.

"We'd have to think real hard about what having a likely criminal on your ticket would say about you."

"It would say I'm the ultimate compassionate forgiver, one who'd make Jesus Christ look like a piker when it comes to turning the other cheek."

"Let's keep the Christ comparisons confined to this room, if you don't mind."

Landon struggled to his feet and started shuffling again.

"VPs don't do a whole lot, so I'm not worried about a crazed gravel plant worker fucking up my presidency. But he'd be an ace on the campaign trail. The ultimate anti-elitist."

Watkins began to knead his chin between his thumb and index finger.

"It *is* possible people might believe he'd be strong on national defense."

"And they'd definitely consider him a straight-talking outside-the-beltway-er."

"Landon and McBride," Watkins said, testing the rhythm. "Landon and McBride."

Landon stopped at the bookcase packed with books he'd never read.

"How about 'Joe Landon: Compassionate Forgiver/Harry McBride: Straight Talker, Straight Man.'"

"We already have the anti-gay vote," Watkins said. "No need to be so blunt. What we'd have to determine—if we're seriously considering something this insane—is whether the millions who allegedly admire Harry McBride would actually feel comfortable with him only a heartbeat from the Oval Office."

Landon turned to Watkins and pointed one index finger at his mask and the other at his butt.

"This is temporary, if you're saying my health would worry people."

"Your injuries might be temporary, but Air Force One going down or an assassin's bullet wouldn't be."

"Unlikely scenarios."

"I agree, but that's how voters think."

Landon returned to his desk and carefully lowered himself into his specially-padded chair.

"I've been in Washington for years, Chris. Most Americans associate that with being out of touch with real people. McBride would counter that perfectly."

"What if he turns out to be completely bonkers?"

"Some of the most powerful, influential leaders in history were completely bonkers."

Each man went into a ponder.

"How we going to find him?" Watkins said, emerging from his first. "The FBI and the state and locals have been useless so far."

"I've got someone on it. Says he's getting close."

"You might want to discuss the legality of having McBride on your ticket with Samuelson first."

"Already have. Samuelson says it's doable."

Watkins threw up his hands in mock defeat.

"You're the boss. Need me for anything else?"

"Not right now."

Watkins stood and looked Landon in the eye, as if still trying to flush out the practical joke.

"I'll call you later about prepping for Meet The Press."

"Sounds good. Never know what curveballs those assholes'll throw."

Landon waited until Watkins left before opening the top drawer of his desk and retrieving a fifth of Johnny Walker Blue; a colleague's token of appreciation for Landon voting aye on an omnibus bill providing infrastructure funds for that senator's state. Landon poured half an inch into a rocks glass, swirled it like a fine wine, and recalled a scene from *Apocalypse Now* as the first sip hit the back of his tongue, the one in which Robert Duvall's character equates the smell of napalm with victory. Landon felt the same way about the blended scotch now filling his mouth, poised to slide down his throat.

Chapter 18

Mary held her index finger to her lips and whispered, "He's a light sleeper" before leading Harry into her mobile home and directing him to sit on a built-in couch padded by worn cushions. She went into the bedroom, and Harry heard her cooing through the thin door as he assessed the trailer, everything in it slightly miniaturized. Mary returned minutes later, her Big Steak uniform exchanged for white sweatpants and a pink t-shirt. An elastic now gathered her hair into a ponytail.

"Your son stay here all alone?" Harry said.

"My mom comes most nights. I'm a nervous wreck 'til I get home when she can't."

"What about a babysitter?"

"Sitters cost money."

Harry noticed a studio photo of a tow-haired infant on the wall, the only decoration other than a dime store mirror and an out-of-date puppy calendar beside the refrigerator.

"Cute kid."

Mary smiled at the photo.

"He's a good boy." She looked from the photo to Harry, her smile melting away. "I'd offer you something, but you probably had enough for tonight."

"Don't think I'll be eating for a week."

Mary filled a mug with water at the kitchen sink and brought it to her guest.

"What's your story, Harry?"

"I'm sure you already know it."

"Only what's in the news."

"There's not much else."

"I don't believe that."

"I wouldn't want to bore you."

"How could being Harry McBride be boring?"

Harry would have laughed if not for Mary's earnest expression and equally earnest tone.

"It's real boring. Believe me."

Mary sat beside him and gestured to the cramped interior.

"I'm a single mom living in a single trailer. Now *that's* boring."

"How old's your kid."

"Just turned four. You have any?"

"No."

Mary's eyes flitted over Harry's bare ring finger.

"A wife?"

"Not anymore."

"Looks like you're free as a bird."

"My cage is just a little bigger than most people's right now."

Mary scrutinized her own cage, as if searching for an escape.

"What's it like on the run?"

"Tiring. Nerve-wracking. I don't recommend it."

"People would have turned you in by now if they weren't on your side. You saw that earlier."

Harry fingered the ridge in his pocket created by his Big Steak winnings.

"They think I'm some kind of rock star."

"Maybe they're living through you, in a weird way."

Harry thought of the miles of Texas still separating him from Mexico.

"They wouldn't want to live through me if I get caught and go to jail."

A pause in the conversation gave Harry time to wonder if Mary wanted something from him.

"I said you could stay here tonight, but I need a favor in return," Mary said, answering the unasked question.

"What kind of favor?"

"I want you to put your hand on my son."

"My hand on your son?"

"On his head."

"Why you want me to do that?"

"For good luck."

Harry noticed Mary's earnestness had returned.

"You must be watching too many of those faith healer shows they got down here."

"I don't believe in that stuff."

"Well, what do you think I can–?"

"I believe in you, though…I not sure why."

Harry noticed his ghostly image reflected by the early morning darkness on the other side of the small window.

"I'm just a gravel worker from Hackettstown, New Jersey," he said, weariness seeping from his muscles into his bones.

"Please, Harry."

Harry wished he hadn't heard the pleading in her voice. He looked at his hands and wondered what they could possibly do for a child, especially one he'd never met.

"All right. If that's what you want."

Mary stood and took Harry into the bedroom. His eyes soon adjusted enough to discern a rumpled duvet draped over a doll-like figure sleeping on a low-slung cot. Mary motioned Harry toward the cot, which squeaked and bowed when he sat on its edge.

"Rest your hand on his head," she whispered. "The one you punched the senator with."

Harry hesitated before cupping his right hand over the boy's forehead. It fit into his palm as snugly as a softball, its warmth easing some of the persistent pain. The boy stirred and Harry smiled down at him–his first smile since Hackettstown. Mary left the room, and time seemed to pass quickly yet slowly from then on. Harry remained on the cot, his hand melded to the child's head while minutes gathered into and beyond an hour, and the blackness enveloping the trailer gradually gave way to tentative light.

Harry soon felt untethered from time and place, from past and future, unchained thoughts and emotions roaming freely in a heightened present. He made no effort to contain them as they transformed Mary's son into the one he and Grace might have had. They roamed even further, until an unexpected love for the sleeping child rose from deep within, powerfully enough to scare him a little.

The youngster opened his eyes just before dawn, neither surprised nor alarmed to find Harry there.

"Ma's gonna buy me an Xbox when I'm five," he said in a small, croaky voice.

Harry had heard of Xbox.

"Xbox, huh? That's good."

"Are you going to be my daddy?"

"Your daddy? Naw, I'm a…I'm just a friend."

"That mean you'll stay with us?"

Harry searched for the right words, careful not to choose any that might disappoint the little guy.

"I'll do my best," was all he could find.

The boy's eyes closed again, and his breathing soon reclaimed a sleep rhythm. Harry looked out the window at the graying sky and knew he should go before it filled with light and the roads filled with cars and watchful eyes. He removed his hand from the boy and kissed his cheek, then left the bedroom and found Mary asleep on the couch. He bent down and kissed her cheek, too, lightly so she wouldn't wake.

He snuck through the kitchen and out into the cool semi-desert. He quietly moved away from the trailer, but stopped after only a few yards and stood as still as the cacti growing from sunbaked ground that felt like concrete through his worn soles. A swallow whistled, the only sound other than Harry's own breathing. He listened to both while fighting the urge to go back inside and somehow save Mary and her son from their difficult, uncertain lives. Because he knew damned well he couldn't save them from anything and would probably only make matters worse if he tried.

So, he took from his pocket the cash he'd won at Big Steak, and returned to the trailer. Yet, instead of opening and stepping through the door, he slipped the money beneath it, then forced himself to turn and walk away, his heart as heavy as his stomach, his tired eyes searching for a car to steal.

Chapter 19

American Wind

There's a feeling in my gut and a song in my heart
inspired by a man who did his part
Ha-rry Ha-rry Mc-Bride
Old Harry took a ride on a strong-blowin' wind
a righteous American wind

Oh, Harry struck out at those with clout
and he made this country shout
Go, Ha-rry, go!
Ride that wind
for us, 'til the end.
Ride it for freedom and for what's right
all through the day and all through the night
to what might
be our country once again.

Now there's a wind sweeping this land
blowing into the sea those that don't stand

for what you and I do
It's cleaning our mountains and scrubbing our plains
whisking away our enemies, giving them well-deserved pain
And Harry's the one who began it all, like a butterfly's wing
starts a squall

Harry, my man, you fill my heart
and you make me want to sing
Go, Ha-rry, go
Ride that wind
for us, 'til the end
Ride it for freedom and for what's right
all through the day and all through the night
to what might
be our country once again

Harry, wherever you may be
I'm pulling for you, brother, as you did for me
You stood up when no one else would
That's what makes you good

Go, Ha-rry, go
Ride that wind
for us, 'til the end
Ride it for freedom and for what's right
all through the day and all through the night
to what might
be our country once again

So go, Ha-rry, go
Ride that wind
for us, 'til the end

Ride it for freedom and for what's right
all through the day and all through the night
to what might
be our country once again
to what might
be our country once again
to what might
be our country once again

Martin Reynolds opened his eyes as the song faded. He turned on his microphone.

"That was Clive Claverdale's "American Wind." Number one song in the nation this week. You youngsters under the age of forty might not know Claverdale was once a classic rocker who fronted a Detroit band called The CC's in the early Seventies. Seems old Clive's reinvented himself as a country singer, which turned out to be a pretty good career move. Stay with me. I'll be back after these commercials."

Reynolds removed his headphones, the "American Wind" refrain repeating over and over in his brain. No surprise, since he'd already played it three times that day, as per management directive. The God-awful tune only reinforced his belief that any song, no matter how bad, could be a hit if force-fed to the masses relentlessly enough.

A minute and a half of commercials remained, enough time to visit the john, one of the few places Reynolds still experienced peace and even inspiration. He managed to find some while standing at the urinal waiting for his stream to start; he decided to give notice at the end of the shift. That third dose of "American Wind" had done it. His flow finally began, and as his bladder emptied, he actually felt grateful to Claverdale and his putrid, cynical, jingoistic song for finally goading him to do what he'd been meaning to for a long time.

"If you're not part of the solution, you're part of the problem," he whispered to the boogered tiles inches from his face.

He finished peeing and went to the sink. He usually looked down at his hands while washing up, a subconscious habit he'd developed to avoid his reflection in the mirror. But he looked directly at his reflection now, without blinking or averting his eyes. First time in years he'd managed to do that.

Chapter 20

Harry pulled onto the shoulder and looked up at the model on the Country Radio KGNC 97.9 billboard, the woman's celluloid face partially obscured by dead bugs peppering the windshield of the Hyundai he'd stolen after leaving Mary in Wildorado.

The land beyond the billboard resembled the backdrop of an old western, a one-dimensional vista of rust-colored buttes and wind-carved boulders. Harry ducked as a car approached and sat up again once it passed. He looked at the model again and realized he'd stopped because she reminded him of Grace.

"Let's go back to that cabin by the lake," he said to her.

The woman's clear blue eyes beamed down through the windshield, her warm smile infused with Grace's brand of hard-earned wisdom. Harry pulled his phone from his pocket.

"You okay?" Grace answered after the second ring.

"I'm fine."

"You shouldn't be using your phone, Harry."

"Hey, remember that steak I cooked up in the Catskills, the one I marinated in olive oil and vinegar and soy sauce?"

"It was good."

"And all them trouts I caught there?"

"They were bass."

"Bass. Right."

"The only thing I caught that day was you."

"I'm still hooked."

"Very funny. I meant how I snagged your leg with my lure."

"Oh, yeah. I still got the scar."

"We had to drive all the way to the hospital to get it out. You were so angry at me."

Harry noticed the billboard model's lips now appeared slightly tighter than before.

"I was probably in pain and—"

"You accused me of doing it on purpose."

"I was just frustrated."

"Why would I put a hook through your leg on purpose? On our freakin' honeymoon!"

Harry began to sweat despite the temperature having dropped along with the sun.

"I don't even really remember it that well."

Grace's voice softened.

"I know you don't. You remember what you want how you want."

Harry imagined the pixilated lips on the billboard tightening even more, until the magical smile had nearly disappeared. He imagined the model's once-smooth forehead pinched into the gentle but effective type of reproach Grace had perfected long ago.

"Let's not argue about fishing and what and how I remember," he said. "We should get back together. Whaddya think?"

"Get back together?"

"I'll figure a way out of this mess and we'll start over. Wipe the slate clean."

"Even if you could get out of your mess, how do we wipe the slate clean? We have a history, ya know, and you have your…stuff."

Harry sensed the desert watching him; he sensed it listening.

"I can be better," he said. "Not so pissed-off and depressed and moody. You can help me."

Grace remained silent, and Harry checked his phone to make sure they were still connected.

"I wish I could," Grace said, finally. *"But the one I really have to help is myself."*

"Which one of your girlfriends told you that?"

"It's just what I need to do for now on."

Harry noticed midnight blue had replaced most of the orange and pink sunset.

"*I* can help you, Grace. We can help *each other.*"

Grace didn't respond at first, then said, *"Plus–and I didn't want to tell you with all this going on–but I been seeing someone."*

That hit Harry in the chest, making breathing difficult.

"It was bass, not trout I caught that day?" he said.

"Did you hear what I just told you?"

"I heard. Who is he?"

"He's a nice man."

"Good for him."

"Who makes me happy."

"Is that all he does?"

"He loves me. He does that, too."

"Do *you* love *him*?"

Grace let out a long sigh.

"I have to go, Harry. So should you."

"I'm gonna call again later."

"Don't."

"Why not?"

"Because."

"Just listen to me, Grace."

"Harry…I'm sorry…So sorry."

Grace hung up, and Harry kept the phone to his ear while staring into the gloom gathering to the southwest.

"I'm glad you're happy," he said to the dead connection. "And I'm glad he's a nice man."

He returned the phone to his pocket just as lightning sprang from a low cloud bank ahead, connecting it to the earth with two malevolent pulses. Harry got out of the Hyundai and looked up at the billboard again, any remaining difference between the model and Grace erased by his mounting fatigue and isolation. He studied her features, searching them for some sort of closure or goodbye. Instead of closure or goodbye, he discovered both eyes had been shot out; small, round holes marking where pupils had been. He spotted another bullet hole piercing the forehead just above the nose.

More lightning jumped from the clouds as Harry scanned the woman's face for further damage, this bolt closer and brighter and followed by a peal of thunder which smoothed into a rumble that rolled over him. He yearned for some sort of guidance to emerge from the weighty hush that followed.

He yearned in vain, and that's when the desert started to close in, transparent walls slowly pressing from all sides. The walls gained speed as they approached, and Harry began to pray for this nightmare to end before the walls squeezed the breath from his lungs and the life from his body. The desert defied his prayers, coming closer and closer, forcing Harry to his knees. He pressed his hands over his eyes and tried harder to wake from his mounting terror before its weight crushed him, before the great rushing nothingness pounced and sucked his soul into perpetual emptiness on the other side.

Chapter 21

Tom Paulus always arrived exactly six minutes late to his own lectures.

This allowed him to stride into the Tulsa Community College Northeast Campus auditorium with all eyes, particularly those of his female students, on him. He wore faded Wranglers this evening, along with a green flannel shirt and the tan corduroy blazer he'd bought in a Salvation Army several years ago. Only leather elbow patches would have given him a more professorial-hip look.

Paulus had already taken a nubby piece of chalk from his pocket. This allowed him to walk directly to the giant, scuffed blackboard and write "HARRY" and "McBRIDE" without hesitating or breaking stride. He then faced the hundred or so students planted in their seats and spent several moments struggling to recall the name of the class he'd have to teach them. *Sociology in the Digital Age.* That's it.

During this pause, Paulus not only recalled which class he'd be teaching, he also had an epiphany, a bright one illuminating the new direction his stagnated career should go in. Instead of devoting only one lecture to Harry McBride and moving on, he decided here and now would be the place and time to start transforming himself into the nation's leading Harry McBride expert. He reasoned that doing so might enable him to ride McBride from perpetual adjunct professor-hood to tenure track, from Tulsa to Princeton, then into bookstores, talk shows, even the lecture circuit.

Of course, Paulus realized Harry McBride as he truly was probably couldn't provide enough material to fuel an entire academic career. He'd have to create that fuel from the blank slate Harry presented, fuel that might not actually exist but would be difficult to refute or disprove. With this settled, he smiled at the young men and women he considered his audience rather than his students.

"Harry...McBride," he said, underlining the name on the blackboard. "Everyone know who he is? Anyone *not* know?"

No hands rose. The class remained silent.

"I'll take that to mean everyone here is aware of Harry McBride. Well, I want to talk about him today. Because, although Harry McBride is clearly just a man, to some he's also an activist. To others he's an insurgent, even a revolutionary. He appears to be a champion and role model to those who support what he did and a villain to those who oppose it. *Fascinating character.* Harry McBride seems to have become a symbol, as well. Let's start there. Any thoughts as to what Harry symbolizes?"

Paulus nodded at a boy who'd raised his hand while still managing to look nearly as uninterested as the others.

"Isn't Harry McBride just a dude, like you said?" the student offered. "I mean, like, wouldn't insisting he's a symbol of something be us projecting our own biases onto him?"

Paulus felt thankful for the softball question.

"I agree HMB is just a *dude*. A *dude* born to a dysfunctional working-class family in Hackettstown, New Jersey. A *dude* who appears to have lived the life someone raised in such a hardscrabble environment would be expected to. But actions make us who we are, and I contend Harry hitting a powerful U.S. senator, possibly our next president, catapulted him above and beyond who he was before that and transformed him from *just a dude* into a symbol. I'll ask again; what's he a symbol *of?*"

Silence.

"This isn't a trick question, people. He can be a symbol of various things, not just one."

A mousy girl seated third row center raised her hand.

"Maybe he's a symbol of anger?"

Paulus pretended to consider the girl's question/statement.

"Anger. Sure. What HMB did was undoubtedly angry. Extremely angry, some might say."

"Rage," another student volunteered.

"Anger. Rage. But what kind of anger? What kind of rage?"

"Violent anger."

Though Paulus found his students' lack of insight and precision annoying, he realized he could use it to his advantage; fill the vacuum they presented with his own conclusions. He noticed many of them thumbing their Androids and iPhones, and suspected most were either texting or checking Facebook or Instagram or that Snapchat thing.

"Obviously, it was violent," he said. "We all saw HMB's fist connect with Senator Landon's nose. We all saw Senator Landon fall from the loading dock. I'm asking what fueled that violence. What instigated and inspired it?"

None dared touch the question, so Paulus gladly forged ahead.

"The answer, quite simply, is Harry McBride's violent anger represents and symbolizes the frustrations of a citizenry disgusted with its elected officials and the elites who control them. Comments? Questions?"

More smartphone checking. Paulus acknowledged the boy in back who'd lifted his hand as if it weighed ten pounds.

"Maybe people're disgusted with their leaders because they don't have good jobs."

"Possibly," Paulus said. "Along those lines, they might be fed up with politicians who they feel are working for the wealthy and for big corporations and for themselves instead of for ordinary Americans who, for some reason, elected them. I believe no one understood this better than HMB did, which is why he seized the moment when it presented itself. That's what visionaries do. That's what revolutionaries do." Paulus jabbed the chalk into the air. "That's what *true leaders* do."

He stopped talking and pretended to contemplate Harry's name on the blackboard before turning to the class again.

"I don't know for sure, but it certainly wouldn't surprise me if HMB is a student of Marx and Lenin and Trotsky. His intentions, even his methods, may very well align with theirs—to overthrow the oligarchy currently running this country and replace it with a system that better serves the average citizen. He's been fairly successful at gaining grassroots support so far, as well as pushback from certain sectors, which may be part of his strategy: reveal enemy positions by drawing their fire. What do you think?"

The students seemed even more fascinated by their hand-held devices now. *Their souls hopelessly mired in a social media abyss,* the adjunct professor thought. He decided to aim his spotlight at a bored-looking young man slumped in the front row, his long, spidery legs sprawled in front of him. Paulus believed this one presented an easy enough target.

"You," he said, pointing at the unsuspecting student. "Comment on what I just said."

The gangly kid looked at Paulus for an unnervingly long time, then smiled from only the left side of his mouth.

"Harry McBride is probably just a guy with ADHD or ADD or some shit like that," he said.

The class erupted into laughter and scattered applause. Paulus grinned to cover his fear of losing the seminar and his irritation at being contradicted.

"Nice counterpoint," he said after the laughter had died down. "Are you a psychiatrist?"

"No."

"A psychologist or mental health counselor or social worker?"

"Naw."

"Okay, have you ever taken courses covering Attention Deficit Hyperactivity Disorder or Attention Deficit Disorder?"

"Nope."

"Well, then, I'd say, with all due respect, you're not exactly qualified to diagnose HMB with ADHD or ADD, or to even speculate whether he suffers from either."

Despite what he considered a successful retort, Paulus couldn't help lamenting his tendency to become enraged whenever his ideas, even those he didn't fully embrace, were challenged. He considered ceding some ground to the boy, perhaps merely entertaining the notion that Harry McBride *could* just be a run-of-the-mill nutter. Paulus realized that would be the Socratic thing to do. He also realized surrendering even a little territory might chip away at the foundation of what he hoped to build on Harry McBride's broad back. He weighed the reality TV dissertation he'd been struggling with for half a decade against the one on Harry McBride he could likely knock out in a year or less. This cemented his decision to stand his ground and bolstered his confidence that the payoff of doing so would far outweigh the ire of these so-called students. He checked his watch and noted with despair that a half hour remained.

"Anyone have more they'd like to add?" he said, hoping no one would.

"You could be right about Harry McBride being a revolutionary," the mousy girl said. "I guess we'll find out."

Paulus directed a patronizing smile her way.

"I guess we will," he said. "Look, it's a nice evening out, so I'm going let you go early to enjoy what's left of it. See you here again Thursday."

Paulus turned his back to the class and again studied the "HARRY" and "McBRIDE" he'd written on the blackboard, the sight of the name conveying nearly the same gravitas for him as "Bruce Springsteen" and "Muhammed Ali" and "John F. Kennedy." He listened to his ersatz audience shuffling out, and turned around when the last had left. He remained alone in the auditorium for several minutes afterward, imagining the now vacant seats occupied by international luminaries and acclaimed academics instead of by disengaged and distracted second-rate pupils. He imagined those seats filled with the world's greatest minds, each there to hear Professor Tom Paulus, PhD explain the significance and the importance and the impact of Harry McBride.

Chapter 22

The first Big Steak Restaurant billboard Calvin Evans spotted filled him with disgust. The next one a few miles later awakened his contempt for those weak and greedy enough to be seduced by its piggish challenge. Each subsequent ad unleashed in him a fresh wave of loathing, not for the steak itself, but for the gluttony and avarice needed to consume it. He considered stopping and finding Bible passages addressing those particular sins, but pressed on instead; he suspected a cash-strapped degenerate like Harry McBride couldn't possibly have resisted the monstrous piece of meat and the $500 reward for eating it.

With eyes aimed straight ahead and un-holstered gun propped against his leg, Evans practiced what he'd say when he finally caught up to McBride:

"Mr. McBride, I assume?...Game over, Harry...You did the crime, friend. Now you'll have to do the time...Please take a knee with me, Harry. Let's pray for your soul together."

He decided to go with that last one when the time came.

The intervals between Big Steak billboards shortened as Evans drove further west, the final one sprouting from the desert only two miles before the actual restaurant. Evans asked himself what Jesus would have done had He been a fallen-from-grace FBI agent turned PI instead of a carpenter. Would He have refused this mission of vengeance or would He have considered the pursuit of Harry to be the pursuit of justice and executed it with zealous vigor?

The concept of justice rarely strayed far from Evans's mind, mainly because of the crucial role it had played in his own fate. Justice, after all, had taken his job at the FBI. Justice had inflicted anger and scorn and shame upon him. Justice had exacted the proverbial eye for an eye. But didn't Jesus, the most just man ever, preach *against* eye for an eye and *for* turning the other cheek? *It doesn't matter,* Evans assured himself. *Your job is to find not judge McBride. And doing so just might lead to your own salvation, your own redemption, your own…second coming.*

His thoughts felt unusually loose, and they soon flowed from his sorry plight to the ancillary role Landon had played in it; specifically to the senator abandoning him when he'd needed his help most. *Hadn't I just saved your daughter from a cult, Joe? Couldn't you have at least reserved judgment of me until after all the facts were in? But don't lose any sleep over poor Calvin Evans. You had your reputation and career to consider. Giving sympathy and support to an accused quasi-pedophile FBI agent might have been political suicide.* Evans pictured the punch he'd seen many times by now, Landon's head snapping back from the blow and his fall from the loading dock. The violent sequence looped over and over in the PI's imagination as he drove, bringing a faint smile to his lips.

Mary looked a tad too old for Evans's taste, much to his relief. Temptation Absent = Temptation Avoided = Trouble Averted.

He smiled politely at the Big Steak hostess and quickly scanned the huge restaurant behind her, as if clues to Harry McBride's whereabouts might be dangling from the steer horns mounted on the walls. He scoped the patrons at the bar next, half-expecting to find Harry working on a steak and a beer amongst them. He didn't look too closely or too hard, though, and for the first time since accepting this gig, he wondered if he genuinely wanted to find the man. This ambiguity caused his heart to sink a little when he spotted the framed photo of Harry mounted on the wall over the giant display steak.

Harry appeared a bit flushed and glassy-eyed in it, but not enough to disguise what had become one of the world's most recognized faces. The accompanying "Harry McBride 9-21-2016" caption dispelled any of Evans' remaining doubts. He moved closer to the photo, and noticed the hostess snuggled on Harry's right side and a waitress snuggled on his left. He also detected smugness beneath the fugitive's smile. *So you ate the goddamned steak and posed with a couple of semi-whores. Big whoop!* Yet, Evans sensed Harry's conquest of the huge slab of beef and his photo session with the girls isn't what truly bothered him. He sensed Harry punching out Landon is what did. Because that's exactly what he wished he'd done years ago. Now McBride's the big shot who punched out the biggest asshole in the US senate, then ate a steak for money, then rubbed up against two hot chicks. *Fuck me!*

Envy and resentment soured Evans's mouth as he stood resenting at the image of Harry while lusting at the image of the waitress cozied up to him, her tanned, toned arm draped over Harry's ape-like shoulders, her glossy-haired head pressed against his barrel chest.

"You wanna eat the steak?" Mary asked.

Evans's eyes dropped from the photo to the massive London broil chilling on its bed of crushed ice. He sized the steak for several moments before facing the hostess.

"Sure, I'll eat the steak."

Evans woke in the emergency room three hours later, wearing a hospital gown, knockout gas still bouncing in his head. A heavyset African-American nurse gave him a disapproving look.

"We pumped your stomach," she said.

"I'll be okay?"

"Not if you keep trying to eat five pounds of meat in one sitting."

"I figure I got about three down. Maybe three and a half."

"That's two pounds too much for a little guy like you."

Evans wondered if she'd glimpsed his wiener during the procedure, if "little guy" referred to *it* rather than to his slender build.

"I would have finished it if I didn't pass out."

The nurse tsked.

"How about the baked potato, the shrimp, the salad, and the Coke? You would have finished them, too?"

"You seem to know the deal over there."

"Honey, Big Steak sends us macho men like you at least once a week."

"That supposed to make me feel better?"

"All's I'm sayin' is used to be we did things in this country. Now we mostly just stuff our faces."

"This happens to be the greatest country on planet Earth, ma'am."

"If you say so." The nurse frowned at Evans's chart. "Your driver's license is Virginia. What you doin' down here in Amarillo?"

"Business."

"What kind of business?"

"You a nurse or a cop?"

"Just askin'."

"If I told you, I'd have to kill you."

"Honey, you look like you couldn't kill an ant."

Evans winched from this fresh blow to his manhood.

"Let me ask *you* something. You know Harry McBride?"

The nurse looked askance at Evans.

"Not personally."

"You probably don't listen to the Grover Budd Show, but Budd calls Harry McBride the blackest white guy since Bill Clinton. You agree?"

The nurse resumed studying Evans's chart, as if trying to determine his soonest possible release.

"Mr. Evans, I got three young kids and a sick mother at home. I ain't got no time to worry if Harry McBride's black as Bill Clinton. Both them's white last time I looked."

"Okay, lemme me ask you this: How black am I? More or less than Harry McBride?"

The nurse gave Evans an incredulous look.

"Why you wanna be black so bad?"

"Because y'all got it goin' on. Because you people aren't all uptight and restricted like us whites."

"You deal in lots of stereotypes, Mr. Evans."

"The way I look at it, you're the free ones now and white people are the slaves…to our own damned selves."

"White folks slaves," the nurse said. "Now I heard it all."

"C'mon. How black am I? Scale of one to ten."

The nurse laughed.

"I don't know about a number, but you're probably the whitest white person *I* ever met."

Evans closed his eyes to better withstand the insult. He examined the paste-colored skin sheathing his forearms when he opened them.

"I'm whiter than the driven snow *and* I couldn't eat the steak. Ain't that the shit." He sat up and dangled his even pastier legs off the side of the examination table. "Can I get outta here?"

"Once the doctor takes a look and says so."

"Well, call him in."

The nurse left the room and the attending physician arrived minutes later. He mumbled his name, checked the chart, then wordlessly examined Evans as if heeding a warning not to engage with him more than necessary. The doctor finally signed a release allowing Evans to leave.

Evans dressed and took a cab from the hospital back to Big Steak. He got in his minivan and looked through the windshield at the sign atop the restaurant depicting a steak resembling the one that had nearly killed him. He then turned on the interior light and again searched for Bible passages regarding gluttony and greed. Unable to find any, he closed the Book and tossed it into the back seat.

"Fuck it," he grumbled. "Fuck Harry McBride, fuck the big fuckin' steak, and fuck *YOU*, Landon!"

His phone rang moments later. "Joseph Landon" on the caller display. Evans's heart began to race and sweat dampened his brow; he wondered if the senator had psychically heard his curse from a thousand miles away. Stranger things had happened. He answered with a fake smile in his voice.

"Hey there, Joe!"

"Any progress?"

"He's practically in my sights."

"Where exactly ARE your sights?"

"Texas. Amarillo."

"Amarillo. A little close to Mexico for my liking. All right, listen up. The nature of your assignment's changing."

Chapter 23

The panorama filling Harry's windshield became increasingly arid as Route 54 curved south and west just beyond the Texas-New Mexico border. The midday sun had strengthened with each passing mile, bouncing heat off the ribbon-like road and roasting the buttes and cacti and deerweed punctuating the land on either side.

Harry turned on the radio while passing through a one gas station town called Carrizozo.

"…Harry McBride is the quintessential coward." Grover Budd's familiar voice riding the only available frequency had become strangely comforting, yet still unsettling to Harry. *"If the early Americans had been anything like Mr. McBride, Texas, New Mexico, Arizona, and California would still be part of Mexico and the frogs would still own Louisiana. You'd be able to fit the U.S. into a shoebox and Canada could invade us whenever it wanted. Where's Grover Budd going with this, you ask. Where I'm going is if Harry McBride was a Republican instead of a Democrat, a conservative instead of an anarchist, he would have taken personal responsibility for his crime instead of collectivizing it by running away and turning his fellow Americans*

into accessories, maybe even accomplices. A true socialist if I ever saw one..."

Harry would have turned off the radio had he not dreaded silence even more than he did Budd. He instead tried to buffer the man by lowering the volume and concentrating on the wide open vista.

"Nice views here, Grace. Like in that IMAX movie we saw at the Museum of Natural History in New York."

You always liked views.

"That's 'cause I got a taste for beauty."

Budd returned after a string of commercials, amped by a double espresso.

"Welcome back to the Grover Budd Show, Americans. Thanks for tuning in. I'm thanking Harry McBride as well, because chances are he too is listening to the most widely syndicated radio show in the nation. If you are, Harry, I challenge you to come to my modest little studio so we can fight it out face to face, man to man, intellectually, of course." Budd sighed. *"Oh, who am I kidding? McBride's too much of a wimp to even call much less visit. I'll offer him another chance. 1-800-757-2900. Give me a holler, Harry, if you have the guts..."*

"He's got a lotta balls calling me a wimp."

Harry fumed for another mile before pulling over and dialing Budd's number. He held for ten minutes before finally getting through to John Willoughby. He spent another five minutes convincing Willoughby of his identity.

Budd picked up during the next commercial break.

"Grover Budd here."

"This is Harry McBride."

"Of course, you are."

"You don't believe me?"

"How do I know for sure?"

"It's me, that's how."

"Our lines are jammed with every imposter in America right now, pal."

"You wanna talk or not? Don't matter to me."

Budd didn't respond right away.

"You do sound the way I imagined. I guess I'll have to trust Willoughby on this. All right, Harry—or whoever you are—we'll be live, so if you happen to blurt something naughty or offensive, we're on a three-second delay."

"All I know is I don't like what you been saying about me."

"Now's your golden opportunity to set the record straight."

"I'll do my best."

"Sounds like a plan…and thanks."

"For what?"

"Never mind. Ready? Here we go. Five, four, three, two, one. Welcome back to the Grover Budd Show, Americans. Make sure you're sitting and not operating heavy machinery. No, Elvis hasn't called in. Even better. After careful screening by moi and John Willoughby, who I consider our very own somewhat flawed Saint Peter, we've determined that the man now on the line is Harry McBride. Swear to God, hope to die. Welcome, Harry McBride. Tell Grover Budd what's bothering you. Tell me what you're just dying to discuss."

"You been asking me to call," Harry said. "*You* tell *me* what we're discussing."

"Fair enough, let's start with how you don't appreciate the things I've been saying about you."

"Well, I don't."

"Can you be a little more specific?"

Harry looked out the window at a thorny cactus with red, plum-sized fruit.

"Because none of what you're saying's even true. You act like you know me or something."

"Oh, but I do know you. Probably better than you know yourself."

"You been telling all these friggin' lies about me, too, to the whole friggin' country."

Budd giggled.

"Historic radio moment, Americans: Harry McBride just semi-cursed on air AND called me a liar."

"Damned straight, I did."

"Then perhaps you should come to the studio and kick my ass for allegedly telling non-truths about you. Violence IS your forte, after all."

"Kicking your ass would be too easy."

"Well, well, well. Seems Harry McBride's suddenly a man of honor."

"I just don't like you calling me a sociologist, or whatever, and saying I hate America and I'm some kinda secret agent."

"Democrat Party agent."

"I'm not that, neither."

"Then who are you?"

"Who am I? I don't know. I'm just a—"

"Better question: WHAT are you?"

"Lemme—"

"And Harry, explain to me and my fellow Americans why you slugged the next president of the United States? Inquiring minds want to know."

Harry had been asking himself the same question since Hackettstown.

"I, umm…yeah, I slugged him…The thing is, he was—"

"Tell us something new. We've all seen The Punch a million times."

Harry wished he could articulate that the content of Landon's loading dock speech, not the inconvenience it caused, is what had triggered his reaction.

"I got a temper, I'll admit, but Landon was chewing up my lunch hour."

"Poor baby."

"I had a roast beef hero in the fridge I wanted to eat."

"So you were han-gry."

"And I'd been on a winning streak at poker I didn't want to break."

"The way you broke Senator Landon's nose and tailbone?"

"I didn't mean to."

"Could have fooled me."

"I know I shouldn't have punched him and all. I regret it and I wish—"

Budd interrupted with faux sniffles.

"Spare us the fake sob story, Harold. Spare us the false remorse."

Harry glanced at the cactus again; its thorns looked as mean as he felt.

"There ain't nothing fake or false about me."

"I agree, Harry. I think you're the real deal. A real deal political operative who's receiving orders from communist China via the Democrat Party. Ever seen the Manchurian Candidate?"

"Who's that?"

"Okay, it's clear to me you don't have any original thoughts or opinions or even basic knowledge of classic American films."

"Hey, I know my movies."

"Then perhaps you can tell us why the Democrats writing your script despise the U.S. so much."

"I went for that Romney guy last time I voted, so I don't know why you think I'm working for Democrats."

Budd went silent, caught by surprise. Recovering, he stammered, *"Mitt Romney? As in Republican Mitt Romney?"*

"They're all a buncha jerks."

Budd sighed again, even more theatrically.

"Americans, it seems my meticulous construction of Harry McBride might be unraveling, crumbling as we speak. NOT! McBride's vote for Romney in 2012—if he did actually vote for Romney—was a strategic ploy to throw us off his trail. Oldest political trick in the book! The man's obviously playing the long game."

"I'm not playing no games."

"Hold that thought, or lack thereof. If you've just tuned in, people, I've got Harry McBride on the line. THE Harry McBride. No joke, no hoax. Harry, have your handlers gone so far as to plant a microchip in your cerebral cortex so they can control you more easily?"

The strain of sparring with Budd had made Harry feel light-headed.

"I'm done here," he said. "I don't have time for this shit."

"I'll bet you don't. You're too busy gunning for Mexico. And watch your language, please. This is a family show."

"Fuck your show, Budd! You can think and say what you want about me. I'm hanging up."

"The old McBride temper, in all its glory. Before you go, Harry, tell us what your next mission is. To help all the Joses and Marias in Mexico cross the Rio Grande so they can register as Democrats?"

Harry pushed the "End" button, and nearly threw his phone out the window. He switched off the radio and seethed behind the wheel until he'd calmed some. He looked at the cactus beside the car once more and this time swore he could see the bright red draining from its prickly fruit. He looked at a yellow deerweed next, and it too began to relinquish its brilliance. The immediate desert and the distant buttes followed suit, slowly exchanging their earthy hues for gunpowder gray. And above, a stark and dreary white gradually replaced what had been a blazing aqua dome.

Feeling the same as the sky now looked, Harry started the Hyundai and pulled back onto Route 54, hoping this great leaching was just another of his panics. He drove on regardless, lack of options pushing him deeper into the fading desert, desperation pushing him deeper into his misery; the only thing that still felt real to him.

Chapter 24

Amarillo, TX (Day 19)

Calvin Evans saw himself stepping through the blue door into that Motel 6 room he'd pictured many times since he'd actually been in it. Though he'd never pictured it as vividly as he was this morning. Nor had he ever felt as doubt and guilt-free about what he'd done there that day. Because the answer to what he'd been asking himself suddenly seemed so obvious: God gave young girls such awesome beauty for a specific reason and an undeniable purpose. *It had to be.* He recalled the firm, queen-sized bed on which he'd given the sixteen year-old the pleasure she'd desired, the patterned easy chair draped with their hastily shucked clothes, the Seinfeld reruns they'd watched on the wide-screened TV afterward. Everything in the room just as it had been that glorious afternoon.

His phone ringing on the night table jolted him from his Alexandria, Virginia Motel 6 reminisce. He breathed easier when he saw "Josh Weinberg" instead of "Joe Landon" on the caller display.

"Josh."

"You owe me another three hundred."

"Am I close?"

"*Depends where you are.*"

"Can't you tell?"

"*You're paying me to track McBride, not you as well.*"

"I'm at a Travelodge outside Amarillo, Texas."

"*Nice there?*"

"Amarillo or the Travelodge?"

"*Forget it. McBride just made a call from Route 54 about five miles south of Carrizozo, New Mexico.*"

"Carrizozo, New Mexico. Sounds like a hoppin' place."

"*Listen to this: He called the Grover Budd Show. It's all over the news, if you haven't heard.*"

"Sounds like McBride hired a publicist."

"*Either that or he's real stupid. So, Route 54 five miles south of Carrizozo.*"

"Got it. Thanks, Josh. Keep it coming."

"*I will as long as you do.*"

Evans hung up and resisted the TV. Because he knew turning it on would only unleash the attractive women undoubtedly waiting for him inside it, women who could easily mesmerize him for hours and distract him from the task at hand. He found female newscasters especially alluring with their long, silky hair and tight, tailored lady-suits. Imagining teenaged girls in those same suits never failed to drive Evans to his lust limit. Be strong, Calvin. *Be very strong.*

He cold-showered, dressed, and escaped the room. Route 40 took him west from the Travelodge, the tundra beyond Amarillo running into cloudless sky that offered no protection from the scorching sun and little diversion from the sex thoughts stalking the PI as relentlessly as he'd been stalking Harry McBride. He merged onto Route 54 after crossing into New Mexico and turned on the radio, but soon turned it off to avoid the sentimental country music dominating the few existing airwaves. He preferred the steady whine of tire against the road that resembled an endless river, the depthless landscape it bisected reminding him of the scene in *Wall Street* in which protagonist Bud Fox stares into the glittery chasm of nighttime Manhattan and asks, *"Who am I?"*

Evans asked himself the same question while staring up the lonesome highway that seemed to be pulling him into the dun-colored desert. He glanced at his reflection in the rearview, searching it for an answer, then looked past his reflection to the Bible he'd tossed into the back seat the night before. The Book made him think of how much his life had changed since he'd embraced Its teachings, enlisted It in his battle against his sinful ways. But has my life improved since then? he wondered. It didn't take him long to conclude that it hadn't, that living virtuously had actually been more difficult than he'd expected. He also wondered if containing his desires for the rest of his days would be too exhausting, perhaps even impossible.

Free of east coast constraints, Evans's thoughts continued to flow, more freely than they had in years, to places they'd never dared venture.

"You there, Lord? You listening? You aware I even exist? Do *You* exist?"

He gripped the wheel tighter just in case a vindictive invisible hand tried to push the minivan off the road.

"Name's Calvin Evans, and there're things I want to know. Firstly, how You doing? Secondly, why all the rules? And thirdly, if I follow those rules, what's my reward? What I mean is what's in it for me?"

He wondered where exactly these God queries were coming from, and how he'd found the courage to ask them. *Change comes slowly until, one day the mountain is reduced to a pile of gravel.* The gravel analogy made him think of Harry

McBride, who he'd briefly forgotten for the first time since Alexandria. A whiptail lizard darted across the road. Evans tapped the brakes to avoid driving over it.

"Was that lizard You, Lord? Sorry, dumb question. You'd be a lion or an eagle, not a lizard. But what I'd really like to know is are all these restrictions I have to obey Yours or did people invent them to control and torture other people? Good people like me."

Evans searched for more creatures or a sign that might give him clues. The only one he saw displayed the speed limit. God's way of telling him he'd live to no more than sixty-five?

"At least answer this: Why'd You make that sixteen year-old girl so incredibly sexy? And am I a sinner for making love to her or did I actually do exactly what You intended me to? Which would mean all the tight-assed Puritans in this country are the ones who've got it wrong."

He kept driving, the sun starting to angle through the windshield into his eyes.

"*ANSWER ME!*" he shouted after adjusting the visor. "Sorry about the outburst, but correct me if I'm wrong: You gave me hunger because You wanted me to eat, right? And You gave me thirst because You wanted me to drink. So, why did You give me desire for hot young girls if You didn't want me to have sex with them? Since we're talking, tell me why the hell You allow blacks to indulge themselves, let it all hang out, while us whites have to play by the rules and obey the laws and walk around like we have sticks up our butts? *It's not fucking fair!*"

The car had drifted while Evans raged, until the right-side wheels found the shoulder. He swerved back onto the road and noticed the gas gauge hovering below the quarter tank mark. He cursed himself for not refilling in Amarillo, and wondered if perhaps his fate entailed getting stranded in the desert like Moses and the Hebrews had. It seemed fitting; he and McBride out in this wasteland, maybe even searching for the same darned thing. Evans began to feel more purposeful, even serene, with his situation in this context.

"You seem unwilling to provide answers, so I'll provide my own," he said. "It's all bullshit, if You want to know what I'm starting to think. I suspect the joke's been on me all along and You're probably laughing Your high holy ass off up there... wherever and whatever *there* is. Not many people have the balls to question You. Well, guess what? I've finally found mine and I *am* questioning You. By the way, not that You care, but Joe Landon can go piss up a stick."

Another whiptail darted into the road. Evans didn't brake fast enough this time, and the car jostled over the prehistoric-looking creature. Evans slowed and looked in the rearview at the mangled reptile writhing against the hot tarmac behind him. The sight sent a chill through his body, and he accidently drove onto the shoulder again. Not good, he thought as he corrected course. He looked in the rearview again, spellbound and horrified by the sight of the mortally wounded lizard. *Not good at all.*

Chapter 25

Senator Landon maintained an extra foot or two between him and each worker he spoke to at the Marion, Ohio Whirlpool plant. He took this precaution despite the presence of his Secret Service detail, just in case anyone tried to go all Harry McBride on him.

He'd discarded his mask the day before, revealing purple, crescent-shaped bruises beneath his eyes. He actually hoped the battle-scarred appearance the bruises imparted would remain until Election Day; he and Watkins had even discussed enhancing them with makeup before deciding the risk of the ruse being exposed outweighed the potential benefits. So, he'd settled for pressing the shiners with his thumbs, just hard enough to keep them from healing.

After working his way down the combustion chamber assembly line, Landon moved to a thrust roller station operated by a beefy, bearded man who reminded him of Harry McBride even more than the others did. He had an uneasy feeling about this one.

"Hi, I'm Joe Landon. And your name is?"

"Don Packer," the worker said, seemingly oblivious to Landon's outstretched hand.

"Nice to meet you, Don."

"Same here, senator. Thanks for taking the time."

"No place I'd rather be."

"Wish I could say the same. Looks like ol' McBride nailed you pretty good there."

Landon retracted his unshaken hand.

"I believe it's commonly known as a sucker punch." He touched beneath his right eye. "You from around these parts?"

"Born and raised. Speaking of sucker punches, I hear Whirlpool might be moving this plant from *these parts* to China next year."

Landon glanced at the trailing reporters and cameramen he now wished would disappear.

"That's the main reason I came today," he said. "To let you boys know I haven't and won't forget about you."

Packer scratched at his ginger-colored beard.

"That's all well and good, senator. But I don't understand why American companies are allowed to ship factories and jobs overseas in the first place."

Landon had been anticipating this type of question and had already formulated an answer that would assure any asker that he opposes offshoring while also justifying the practice *and* concealing the role he'd played in enabling it.

"I realize Whirlpool relocating this plant to China might seem a bit harsh and unfair, Don. Don't get me wrong, I'm one hundred percent against it. That said, the economic theory behind the move, if it does happen, is absolutely sound. You see, freedom from overbearing government regulations is the bedrock of capitalism which, as you know, is the engine of our economy." Landon shifted his tone from 8th to 5th grade level. "I think we can both agree that in order to sell their products to Americans like yourself for an affordable price, Whirlpool has to manufacture them as cheaply as possible. Since labor and materials cost less in China, Whirlpool actually owes it to the citizens of this nation to move its factories *there* so it can keep its prices low *here*."

Landon had intended to nail home his point by asking Packer whether he himself would manufacture in China if he had the awesome responsibility of running a huge public company like Whirlpool. Packer jumped in before Landon could.

"Senator, I'm just a line worker in a washing machine factory, so what the hell do I know? But dontcha think a company that uses America's freedom and protections and economic system to make billions should show some loyalty to the country and employees who made it possible? I mean, we're the ones who do the work."

Landon glanced at the cameras and mics hovering a little too close for his comfort.

"You raise a valid point, Don. Again, if elected president, I assure you I'll do my very best to stop corporations like Whirlpool from manufacturing overseas."

Packer smiled, and a knowing glint came into his eyes.

"I'm sure you will. Ya know, I been reading some U.S. companies even get tax breaks for offshoring. *Tax breaks* for offshoring. It's like they're being rewarded for it."

Landon's nose began to tingle, as if anticipating another blow.

"It's a little more complicated than that in reality."

"I also watch a fair amount of TV," Packer said. "Even C-Span once in a while."

"C-Span's an excellent channel."

"Boring as hell, but it helps me keep tabs on what you politicians are up to."

Sensing where this might be going, Landon offered his hand to Packer again.

"It's been a pleasure, Don. Keep doing what you're doing. America needs hard-working men like Don Packer. Can I count on your vote in November?"

Packer let Landon's hand hang a second time.

"I might be just a blue-collar nobody," he said, steel in his voice now. "But I'm a blue-collar nobody who actually reads the Congressional Record from time to time."

"Well, what do you know?"

"One thing I know is you voted *for* laws giving tax breaks to offshoring companies," Packer said, ignoring the rhetorical nature of Landon's question. "Another thing I know is you voted *against* laws meant to prevent it."

Landon glanced at his Secret Service detail.

"Let me explain something, Don."

"You can start by explaining the Creating American Jobs and Ending Off-shoring Act S. 3816. Whirlpool wouldn't even be thinking of moving this plant to China if it had passed. You might not remember, but you voted against that particular bill."

"Can you comment, senator?" one of the reporters asked.

"Mind your own business," Landon snapped at the reporter before focusing on Packer again. "I think you've misunderstood my philosophy and my intentions, Don."

"Your philosophy and intentions are probably gonna put me out of a job pretty soon. Which reminds me. You opposed extending unemployment benefits every time it came to vote during the recession. That happens to be in the Congressional Record, too."

"Now you're getting into fiscal policy, which is an entirely different matter."

"Senator, everyone knows big companies like Whirlpool line your pockets in return for all kinds of breaks and unfair advantages. It's no secret. You call it capitalism. I call it corruption."

"*Corruption?* That's a loaded term."

Packer shook his head with resignation.

"You must think we're all a buncha dumbasses."

"I don't think that at all."

"Actually you do. And, for the most part, you're right. Which is why you'll probably win in November."

Packer abruptly turned his back to Landon and resumed working, as though the candidate had never been there. Landon waited until his nerves had settled before moving on to the next potential voter. He hoped the dull roar of the machines had obscured most of his conversation with Packer. He wondered if he could convince the reporters to edit it out entirely.

"Hi, I'm Joe Landon," he said to a man at a station down the thrust roller line from Packer, having already decided to call Calvin Evans again after leaving Whirlpool, check on his progress finding Harry McBride.

Chapter 26

Calvin Evans had regained most of the bravado he'd lost after flattening the whiptail an hour earlier, though an ill-defined unease still buzzed him like a mosquito.

"Do we need to talk about it?" he said, watching the road for more wayward lizards. "Probably not, since You supposedly know everything. I'll tell You anyway: I'm not sorry about what I did with the girl at the Motel 6. There, I said it. *You* created that apple and *You* tempted me to eat it. Your fault, not mine. Would I do it again? Damned straight, I would. It was like eating a ripe peach, which is even sweeter than an apple. I'm allowed to eat peaches or are they also on Your forbidden list?"

No longer expecting divine answers, Evans surveyed the sun-burnt desert and wished the rest of America possessed the same stark purity, the same, what's the word?...*integrity*. He wondered how a nation so crammed with garbage and junk, with pointless emails and texts, with nasty tweets and posts and memes, with bad TV and even worse music, could still be God's favorite. Not that it mattered to him so much anymore.

His phone rang and his mood only worsened when he saw "Joseph Landon" on the caller ID display. He recalled once more how Landon had abandoned him in his darkest hour.

"Evans here."

"Any luck?"

"He made a call near a relay tower a bit south of me."

"Where's that?"

"I just passed Ancho, New Mexico."

"Well, put the pedal to the metal."

"I'm doing the best I can."

"Do better, if you don't mind."

"Instant gratification," Evans muttered.

"What's that supposed to mean?"

"It means we live in a society that demands everything right away and throws out what it no longer needs."

"Disposables represent a large segment of our GNP, not that I have time to give an economics lecture."

"You're absolutely right, Joe. Disposable razors, disposable napkins, disposable *people*."

"I don't have time to give a civics lecture, either."

"I'd call it history, not civics."

Silence on the other end. Then, *"I'm paying you good money, don't forget."*

"Is there such thing as good money?"

"Sounds like you've been reading too much Bible lately."

"You should try it yourself some time."

"Or maybe it's the Communist Manifesto you're studying."

"I've actually been attempting to think independently, for a change."

"How's that working out?"

Evans resisted the urge to hang up.

"You really believe McBride can help you win the election?"

"Got a better idea?"

"People will see through it."

"I doubt that."

"But are you going to discard McBride like an empty soda can if I turn out to be right?"

"You just do what I hired you to. I'll worry about the rest."

Evans lowered the window and wished the hot air invading the car could blow away everything linking him to Landon. He summoned an extra dose of courage, then said, "I might not be perfect, Joe. Far from it. But I *am* the man who saved your daughter. *Don't you ever forget that."*

"And don't *you* ever forget you were just doing your job."

"Hey, Joe, are you hungry?"

"Am I hungry? Sure, I could eat something."

"Good. Then why don't you take a big bite of *GO FUCK YOURSELF?"*

Evans hung up before Landon could respond. The senator didn't call back and Evans kept driving toward the darkening horizon. He saw lightning flash over a distant butte. Few things frightened him more.

"Testing me again, Lord? You put me through all kinds of shit and still demand my allegiance and unconditional love. How about *You* show some love, for a change? At least throw me a bone once in a while. You can start by turning off the storm."

The next bolt made Evans jump in his seat.

"That was *close."*

More electricity hit the ground moments later, this time less than a mile ahead. Evans considered U-turning, but his rearview reflected the same darkness that lay ahead, as if the storm had outflanked and encircled him. His nervousness deepened into full-blown fear, and sweat dampened his face and palms. He drove in a semi-trance now, imagining the storm sucking the car into its maw.

The next lightning struck a mere hundred yards away, and Evans spotted something in the road as the flash cleared from his vision. He couldn't be sure what it was until he'd gotten to within thirty feet of a snake that had slithered from the desert to absorb residual heat from the tarmac before night fell.

A shivering rattle sprouted from the coiled viper's tail, and a whip-like tongue darted between its thin, hard-looking lips. Evans stopped and watched the creature, unsure if he should drive over or around it. The rattler finally lifted its head and aimed its bulging black eyes directly at the PI, as though daring him to look away.

Evans tried to, but the snake seemed to have reached into the car and hijacked his will. Evans began to shake, gently at first, then violently. His urine soon started to flow, but he felt no shame, sure any normal human confronted by Satan would piss themselves, too. He never did come with horns and pitchfork, did he? No, he came as a new "friend" or a sexy, slightly under-aged girl. Other times as a rattlesnake in the New Mexico desert. Either way, Evans knew Satan had found the opening his questioning of God had provided, striking as soon as Evans presented it on a silver platter.

He retrieved the Bible from the back seat and turned to Psalm 23:4. His voice trembled along with his hands as he read it aloud:

"Yea, though I walk through the valley of the shadow of death, I will fear no evil; for You are with me; Your rod and Your staff, they comfort me."

He felt stupid and lazy for choosing such a familiar, oft-read and quoted passage. He also felt like a traitor and a fraud for having questioned then beseeched the Lord. He judged himself as harshly as he once did those who only embraced Him from their deathbed. But he could think of no other option as he closed the Book and let It slip from his fingers into his pee-soaked lap.

Another lightning bolt struck, this one only yards away. Evans screamed along with its deafening thunder. Yet, he felt surprisingly calm afterward, newly aware that being forsaken by the Lord may have also released him from all His onerous controls and restrictions. Evans also realized he had nothing left to lose now that his ties to the so-called Almighty had clearly been severed. He smiled as his terror retreated before this new-found freedom, no longer frightened by God or fate or even by Satan eyeballing him from the road, his tongue tasting the air as if measuring the distance between them.

Chapter 27

John Willoughby seemed surprised when Grover Budd asked him about his weekend plans. They rarely discussed anything personal.

"Probably bring the kids to the water park out in River-head," Willoughby said.

"Sounds fun."

"They've been bugging me to take them before it gets cold. How about you?"

Budd had nothing scheduled, at least nothing wholesome like taking children to a water park.

"Not much," he said. "Little this, little that."

"You could come with us, if you want."

"Haven't been to a water park since I was a boy."

The conversation had sparked a memory that took Budd back to Water World, in Grand Island, Nebraska, to the twisty-turny tube he'd ridden there so many years ago. It put him right into the swooping wet darkness preceding the burst of sunlight just before the liquid embrace of the dolphin-shaped pool at the bottom. Budd drew a blank trying to recall the last time he'd had as much fun; true fun, not the vodka-fueled kind.

Willoughby tapped his watch before Budd could ask him what time he'd be going to the park. He lowered the headphones over his ears.

"Welcome back to the Grover Budd Show, Americans. Where was I? Socialism, terrorism, threats to your freedom, work camps. *Work camps!* That's where we left off before my esteemed sponsors kindly gave me a pee and poo break. Here's the latest on those work camps: my sources say our beloved president still plans to build them even at this eleventh hour of his 2nd term. He plans to build them way up in North Dakota, which closely resembles what part of the world? That's right, folks. *Siberia.* Burrr! And although they'll be called work camps and, believe me, there'll be lots of work done up there, they'll actually be re-education camps. Suppose you happen to think unrestricted free market capitalism is the best route to prosperity for the greatest number of people. Well, that don't jive—I mean *jibe*—with what our president and his minions believe. So, they might just ship you off to sunny North Dakota and keep you there until you see things their way. Which means until you believe government should control the economy and, by extension, your life. They'll reprogram the hell out of you until you actually *want* government to dictate your healthcare choices and decide when to euthanize your granny and abort your fetus. Oh, they'll break you down until you roll over and say, 'Uncle Sam, please take half my hard-earned pay and redistribute it to a bunch of illegal aliens and welfare mamas...'"

Budd's mind had wandered back to Water World as he spoke, this time depositing him atop the massive yellow beach ball sitting like a giant egg yolk in a shallow pool. He saw himself and the other kids pulling themselves up the ropes tethered to the pole protruding from that overgrown inflatable, then bouncing down its sides into the water. He also pictured the towering slide, visible from miles away. The thing dropped at a nearly forty-five degree angle, the sign at the top warning riders to cross their legs before going down. Grover never dared to.

"…and where does Harry McBride fit into all this, Americans? A rhetorical question, since the answer should be obvious to anyone with half a brain. What's scary to me, what I find *truly* frightening, is Harry's little political publicity stunt actually seems to be working. Only in America, home of the brave, land of the free and, unfortunately, of millions of nincompoops, can a man like McBride become an icon. I mean, did you hear there's a Harry McBride Society now? Some colleges are offering Harry McBride courses, for Christ sake! They're even staging Harry McBride punch-out contests. And get this: the number one song in the nation right now is called *American Wind,* which is about none other than Harry McBride. Lord have mercy on us…"

Budd had been trying to think only of the slides and pools at Water World. But his thoughts inevitably went to the girl he'd seen there that day. She must have been ten or eleven, roughly the same age as the young Grover, who'd followed her most of the afternoon, making sure to be on all the same lines as she. Her cuteness rather than her still-dormant sexuality is what had attracted him–how adorable she'd looked in her teal one-piece swimsuit, her hair braided into short pigtails, a perfectly straight part dividing her plum-shaped head.

The girl didn't respond or react when Budd finally found the nerve to speak to her while they waited to go on the flume. Only her lids fluttered as she watched him with her big, brown eyes, seemingly too stunned to blink. Budd said hello again, and the girl's continued silence is what cut him, deeply, morphing in his tender, adolescent mind from normal pre-teen shyness to outright rejection.

Budd had already fallen into what he referred to as The Zone, a mental state that allowed him to practically sleep-talk through his shows. He'd periodically wake from these semi-conscious slumbers just long enough to gauge his progress and correct course, if necessary. He closed his eyes as he rambled about Harry McBride while trying in vain to forget the Water World girl and her rebuff after all these years. He wondered why such a minor wound had festered and refused to heal.

"…What really irks me, Americans, is this Harry McBride fraudster has even become a sex symbol. In other words: *chicks dig him*. Maybe he represents the macho man of action that's almost extinct in our wimpified culture. I'd say clocking a sixty-two year-old man without warning is hardly macho, but you ladies believe and feel what you want. Grover Budd can't stop you. Nor can any amount of logic, since logic and women usually don't see eye to eye. Sorry, gals, but it's true. Then again, what the hell do I know about women? I'm no Harry McBride. I'm just a balding, overweight radio personality…"

Budd had long contemplated getting hair implants and joining a gym to rectify those two flaws. A TV career would have left him little choice. But radio had allowed him to delay action on his appearance and sub-par physicality; he'd always suspected a full head of hair and a slimmer build wouldn't make him much more attractive, anyway.

"…Frankly, I can't wait until they finally catch McBride and throw him in jail. Because even *I'm* sick of talking about him. But talk about him I must, since he undoubtedly represents the single greatest threat to America in my lifetime. So, it's my duty to warn you, to educate you, to *protect* you…"

Budd opened his eyes and noticed Willoughby signaling a toilet run: his left-hand pinky crooked through the circle he'd created by pinching together his right-hand thumb and index finger. Budd nodded, closed his eyes again, and tried to summon enthusiasm for going to Peacock Alley after the show. But the prospect of hiring a girl didn't excite him as much as it normally did. Today it felt more like habit or routine, like drinking coffee in the morning or watching a sitcom rerun before bed. Budd knew he'd go to the Peacock regardless, his decision made by not deciding against it. He realized he'd stopped talking; cardinal sin for a radio host.

"Excuse the silence, Americans. Fell into deep thought there, which can be a real curse. Sometimes I wish I never did it. My life would be so much easier and my soul would be free instead of caged and tormented by passion and caring. Apathy is bliss, my friends. That's why we're one of the happiest countries on earth. U.S. of A. United States of Apathy. So what if an undercover Democrat Party operative named Harry McBride punched out one of our finest senators and our most promising presidential candidate? Who cares if ol' Harry's trying to start a revolution that will destroy our way of life? Let's not only admire the hell out of him, let's turn him into a hero, a sex symbol, a real salt of the nation. *Assault* of the nation's more like it…"

Budd checked his watch, concerned Willoughby would still be reading the NY Post on the can when the next commercial break came. He felt especially tired and disconnected today, and he sensed depression preparing to attack, as it did from time to time. The control room door finally opened, and Willoughby settled back behind his console.

"Anyway," Budd continued, struggling to re-connect with his stream. "Harry McBride. What else can I say? What else can I do? Keep listening, Americans. I'll return after these."

Willoughby cut to commercials, and Budd leaned back in his chair. He looked up at the ceiling, and his mind went blank as he studied the tiny holes in the sound-proofing tiles.

"You okay, Grover?"

"I'm fine. Just tired."

"Well, you have the weekend after this."

The weekend. That empty, yawning gap between Friday evening and Monday morning.

"Yeah, I'll rest up."

"Let me know if you change your mind about the water park."

Budd thought of the young girl again, of how sweet she'd looked in her one-piece. He now saw the pink beads tied into her pigtails. He'd forgotten about them.

"I'll let you know," he said, depression creeping closer because he knew he'd never find the guts to go to another water park.

And while still picturing those pink hair beads, he finally quit wondering why the girl didn't answer when he'd spoken to her. He understood she'd seen right through him that day, to his true essence. It made perfect sense now.

"Ten seconds," Willoughby said.

Budd pulled his eyes from the ceiling and leaned into the mic. He watched Willoughby mark off the final four by folding the fingers of his right hand.

"Welcome back, Americans. I'm sure most of you stayed with me, but for those just joining, I was talking about Harry McBride...."

Chapter 28

An unusually subdued-sounding Grover Budd had accompanied Harry through the storm and into southern New Mexico. Harry kept listening only because he felt his very existence at this desolate edge of the nation somehow depended on Budd still talking about him.

Route 54 took him past another Harry McBride Society billboard, the donation request of $2 rather than $1 the only variation from the others he'd seen. A green sign on the far side of a tiny town called Chaparall indicated only five miles of America remained. Harry checked the odometer and decided to go another three before turning onto one of the unmarked dirt tracks intersecting 54 every so often. He planned to follow the track into the bush and wait for darkness before abandoning the car and sneaking across the line on foot.

He maintained a steady fifty-five to avoid attracting attention, too anxious to look behind or very far ahead. He tried not to think of Grace, either, the likelihood of never seeing her again almost too much to bear. An object ahead provided welcome distraction from his angst. He thought it might be a hit deer or armadillo until he got closer and it became a car on its side, steam wafting from its crumpled hood.

Harry glided to a stop just shy of the overturned vehicle, its exposed undercarriage reminding him of a disemboweled beast. He got out and approached the car. Through the front window he saw the driver, whose chest had collapsed around the steering wheel, her face frozen in a contorted death mask. The scent of whiskey teased Harry's nostrils, and he noticed glass sprinkled like party glitter over the woman's broken body, the labeled portion of a shattered Jack Daniels bottle draped across her hip. He reached in and touched beneath her jaw. No pulse, only cool skin over stiffening muscles.

Movement on the shoulder of the road drew Harry's attention to a blank-faced little girl standing beside a sage bush, blood streaking her forehead and trickling from her nose. Welts and dirt scuffed her cheeks and her bare, stick-like arms. Harry went to the child, treading slowly and lightly to avoid frightening her.

"What's your name, sweety?"

The girl didn't answer.

"You okay?" Harry crouched before her. "You hurt?"

Still no answer.

"The lady in the car. She your mommy?"

The girl's frightened eyes brightened at the mention of her mother, making Harry feel even worse.

"How old are you, little one?"

She held up three tiny fingers.

"Three, huh. You're a big girl, aren't you?"

Harry thumbed away the blood beneath her nose and stood. The child looked even smaller and more helpless from this vantage. She wore only one sneaker, the pinky toe of her unshod foot poking through a tattered sock. The temperature had dropped now that only a wisp of daytime remained in the highest part of the western sky. Harry positioned himself between the girl and the wind and tried not to think too hard or too long about what to do next. For he knew that would only prevent him from doing it. He finally took his phone from his pocket and dialed 9-1-1.

"*Phone number, please,*" asked the operator.

Harry's mouth and throat had gone dry, making it difficult for him to speak.

"*Phone number, please.*"

"It's 201-462-0813."

"*What's the emergency?*"

"Car accident. One dead and a kid who needs help."

"*Location of the accident?*"

"Route 54, about four miles north of Mexico."

"*Your name, sir?*"

Harry's mouth dried even more, nearly fusing his tongue to its roof.

"*I'll need your name, sir.*"

Harry looked south toward the border and imagined he could actually see it. He licked his lips and struggled to swallow.

"Name's Harry."

"*I'll need a last name, too.*"

Harry looked down at the girl through welling tears.

"It's Mc…It's McBride…It's Harry McBride. This is Harry McBride calling. *You got that?*"

He ended the call before the operator could ask more, then squatted before the girl again. He considered putting her in the Hyundai to keep her warm, but thought better of it.

"Don't worry, kid, you're safe with me," he said, pulling her close to him. "You're safe with Harry McBride. Harry McBride won't let nothing happen to you."

The wind had started to whistle past the tailpipe of the wrecked car, its cold reawakening the ache in Harry's right hand. He soon heard a vehicle approaching from the north, and Calvin Evans's Caravan appeared in the distance. The minivan slowed as it came closer, and it angled to a stop across both lanes several yards away. Evans got out and faced the man he'd been chasing for so many miles.

"McBride?"

Harry stood again.

"Who's asking?"

Evans didn't answer; he just kept looking at Harry, seemingly engaged in a fierce internal debate.

"I'm nobody," he said, finally. "Just a fellow citizen."

Harry indicated the overturned car with his chin

"I called 911. The mother's in there."

Evans glanced at the wreck, then closed his eyes and lowered his head.

"To escape all these things that shall come to pass, and to stand–" He stopped mid-sentence.

"What's that mean?" Harry said.

Evans opened his eyes again and smiled, almost apologetically.

"Nothing. An old habit. I'd get the hell out of here if I was you."

Harry gathered the girl against his legs.

"I can't leave the kid."

"I'll look after her."

"How can I be sure?"

"You can trust me, Harry. Probably more than anyone else."

Harry looked down at the girl again and hesitated before releasing her.

"You wait here with her," he said to Evans.

"I will. Now get going."

Faint sirens had joined the wind by now; a lone-some-sounding duo accompanied by flashing cherry tops that crested a low rise to the south minutes later. Evans watched the two cop cars and turned toward Harry when they'd closed to within a mile. But only Harry's footprints leading across the shoulder into the desert remained. Evans wished he could have said goodbye and wished Harry luck. He wished he could have shaken his hand and told him something wise and profound that he could take with him. He quickly kicked dirt over the footprints before lifting the girl and holding her tight as together they watched the approaching cherry tops grow larger and brighter, and together they listened to the sirens get louder.

And from behind a sandstone boulder less than a hundred yards off the road, Harry made sure an officer had put the girl safely into his cruiser before turning and continuing on into the desert that dusk had shrouded in gauzy blue. His body started to feel buoyant as he walked toward Mexico, a surreal weightlessness that allowed his feet to merely skim the hard, pebbly ground. He imagined his feet leaving the earth entirely and his body floating like a helium balloon above it. He imagined that until he felt he *was* floating, peddling the air in a semi-dream he had no desire to wake from. In it, he saw the cop cars flashing red, white, and blue beneath him, then the entire desert as he rose farther into the welcoming sky. He kept rising and soon saw the whole nation, stretched from New Jersey to California, from Montana to New Mexico. He saw the forests and the plains, the mountains and the rivers, the small towns and the big cities. He saw it all from on high where he knew no one could touch him, feeling almost happy for the first time he could remember.

I'm a bird above America
and over the border I'll go
I'm free, Grace, at least for now
Maybe I'll just keep flying
One day I'll show you how

Acknowledgements

With thanks to Shelley Simmons-Bloom, Joan and Robert Bloom, Jonathan Bloom, Bunny Simmons-Bloom, and also to Alexandra Shelley for her invaluable editorial expertise and insight.

About the Author

Matt Bloom has worked many jobs over the years to support his writing habit, including but not limited to kitchen hand, freight elevator operator, migrant laborer, truck driver, bartender, and currently as an anti-money laundering investigator. Matt grew up on Long Island and has lived briefly in Australia, Mexico, upstate New York, and Ohio. He now lives in Manhattan with his wife, Shelley Simmons-Bloom, and their cat, Bunny. Matt's first published work of fiction was a short story in the Westside Spirit, a free weekly newspaper that still exists. His three previous novels are Blue Paradise (1998), A Death in the Hamptons (2002), and The Last Romantic (2005). His children's books are Hello, My Name is Bunny! (2016) and Hello, My Name is Bunny! London (2018). Matt has also earned fiction fellowships at Sewanee Writers' Conference (1998), Breadloaf Writers' Conference (1999), and a residence at MacDowell Artists' Colony (2003).

Made in the USA
Columbia, SC
07 April 2019